John Harrison

On the Primitive Mode of Making Bishops

John Harrison

On the Primitive Mode of Making Bishops

ISBN/EAN: 9783337395629

Printed in Europe, USA, Canada, Australia, Japan

Cover: Foto ©Andreas Hilbeck / pixelio.de

More available books at **www.hansebooks.com**

ON THE

PRIMITIVE MODE OF MAKING BISHOPS:

BEING

AN ENQUIRY AS TO WHETHER THEY WERE CREATED
CHIEFLY BY THOSE OVER WHOM THEY WERE
TO PRESIDE, OR BY ONE OR MORE OF
THEIR OWN ORDER.

BY

JOHN HARRISON,

VICAR OF FENWICK, NEAR DONCASTER, AUTHOR OF
"WHOSE ARE THE FATHERS," ETC.

Quando ipsa (plebs) maxime habeat potestatem vel eligendi dignos sacerdotes, vel indignos recusandi.—CYPRIANUS, EPISTOLA LXVII.

LONDON:
LONGMANS, GREEN, AND CO.
1870.

ON THE PRIMITIVE MODE OF MAKING BISHOPS, &c.

THIS is a question of considerable importance at the present time, and the conclusion come to, in proportion to its definiteness, may tend to determine whether the Church of England is still to be considered, by "consanguinity of doctrine," a sister of the Reformed Churches which now hold substantially the same doctrine (as the Church of Scotland, to wit), or, by virtue of a discipline claimed to be essential to the existence of a Church of Christ, she is not rather a branch of that stock which contains the corrupt and unreformed Greek and Roman Churches. Many of those who take the latter view complain of the isolation of the Church of England, and sigh for union with one or both of those Churches, but regard all other bodies of Christians, however enlightened and influential, as forming no part of the Church of Christ, and every member of such bodies as being virtually "a heathen man and a publican" in relation to it. The practical bearing of our question at the present time is of no little importance, and the fact that it is before Convocation may give an additional interest to its discussion. But before entering upon it, it is necessary to premise one or two points which will be found stated and proved in my book entitled "Whose are the Fathers?" Indeed, there is little in this paper which may not be found in that larger work. My apology for reproducing any portion of it, is, that it is far easier to disseminate a few pages than a bulky volume, and where I may obtain seven readers for the latter, I may obtain seventy and seven for the former.

The holy Apostles founded churches wherever they could, and to each they constituted or ordained a plurality of elders, presbyters, or bishops. It is to be presumed that in every Church there was a presiding presbyter or bishop. In the year 250, in North Africa alone, there were about seven hundred churches or congregations, each with its plurality of presbyters, and each having a president, to whom now was given the exclusive title of bishop. Cyprian was such an one, though more ordinarily called by a title of office (*præpositus*) common to the presbyters, and whom he was in the habit of addressing as fellows (*compresbyteri*). Cyprian claimed for himself, and others in the like office, to stand in the same relation to their fellow presbyters as St Peter was considered to stand in relation to his fellow Apostles. It is not at all necessary in the present inquiry to determine whether a bishop is the first among his equals, or is as much above a presbyter as a presbyter is above a deacon. Good Bishop Hall zealously and conscientiously held the latter view, as many of our clergy now do.

That there may be no misapprehension of the question to be considered, it shall be substantially stated in a borrowed form. " (1) Did Christ frame a scheme of government, and leave it as a charter to the body of those who believed in Him, and give it in charge to His followers at large to fill up the offices constituted in that scheme? (2) Or did He empower a college of selected persons to act in the offices which He established, and intrust to them plenary powers of government over the society? (3) Or did He even go farther than this, and by instituting the society in their persons, thus restrict himself to its virtual or potential, and leave them its actual or historical formation? (4) If so, were the powers of those persons wholly or in part transmissible, (5) or were they to expire with their lives? . . . (6) They were to continue, even to the end of the Christian dispensation." (*Church Principles, by W. E. Gladstone, Esq.*, pp. 192, 205, A. D. 1840.) The last questions, the fourth and fifth, followed by an affirmation, are the points with which we are more especially concerned. It will be maintained in this paper that, according to the records of the early Church, bishops received their power of office, whatever it was, from the laity by their election of them, and that "the Apostolic office," to use the language of the learned Barrow, "according to its nature and design, was not successive or communicable in perpetual descendance from them, was not designed to continue by derivation, and which no man, without gross imposture and hypocrisy, could challenge to himself;" and that the attempts to give proof of it by some modern high Anglicans are worthless, if not contemptible.

We shall maintain first, as proposed, that primitive bishops, such as we have already described, received their power of office from the laity by their election of them. In support of this will be adduced the testimony of a most learned Roman Catholic commentator, Alphonsus Tostatus, Bishop of Avila, who lived about 100 years before the Reformation. Following very much the method adopted by Theodoret in his exposition of Holy Scripture, he raises a question upon the account given of the man who had been found gathering sticks on the Sabbath day, and who is said to have been brought "unto all the congregation, and they put him in ward." (Num. xv. 33, 34.)

"*Whether a community or a church can have the exercise of jurisdiction, and whether Christ gave the keys especially to Peter only, or to the whole Church, and how the authority of the keys is transferred from one prelate to another.*"

To this he answers, "It should be observed that this putting in ward is not referred to the whole multitude, for it had not jurisdiction itself, since jurisdiction as to action cannot be suitable to a society, but to a person to whom it is restricted; for jurisdiction requires action, so as to rule and command. But since a society is not properly any one thing, but by accident, as a heap of stones, it cannot perform any acts: therefore it is impossible that jurisdiction as to action be in a society.. Yet jurisdiction in regard to its origin and power belongs to the society; for all persons receiving jurisdiction, receive it by virtue of the society, for it cannot itself judge by itself. But not to a society only, but it appears thus concerning the keys of the Church, for they were given by Christ to the whole

Church. But, however, the whole Church could not dispense them, since it was not some one person. He delivered them to Peter, in the name of the Church. If, however, it should be understood that the keys were delivered specially to Peter, not only would an unsuitable consequence follow, which is, that the other apostles would not have any authority of the keys, and that would be untrue, for to them was given the power of remitting sins, as appears from the 20th chapter of John, namely, 'Receive ye the Holy Ghost: whose soever sins ye remit, they are remitted unto them; and whose soever sins ye retain, they are retained.' Yet this power alone is a key; therefore the other apostles received the keys. But still there was another inconvenience greater, namely, that when Peter was dead, the keys would not remain, which would necessarily follow, if they were given to Peter only. And if they were not also given specially to himself alone, but also to all the apostles, when they were dead the keys would not remain in the Church; for these apostles had not the power of giving the keys to others, and making them their successors, since no one can make a prelate a successor to himself; and yet all successors of the blessed Peter and other bishops have the keys, as Peter and the other apostles had them; therefore the keys were not given to them as to persons to whom they were restricted, but as ministers of the Church; and then the keys were rather given to the Church than to them; and in this manner the keys could never cease from the Church, since the Church which has them radically never dies. Then it would evidently appear that when the blessed Peter was dead other chief pontiffs might succeed to equal power, because that power of the keys was in the Church, and because the Church could not dispense it, since she was not one person, the jurisdiction of the keys was delivered to Peter as a person elected to the use of that jurisdiction, and because, when the blessed Peter was dead, the Church, still always having the keys, could elect a successor to him, and by electing confer the same power which Peter had; nor would it be necessary on the death of the blessed Peter, that Christ should again confer the keys on his successor, which, however, would be necessary if the keys had been given exclusively to Peter, or exclusively to the other apostles, and not to the Church. . . . . Thus far it appears, when a see is vacant, the chapter have all things which belong to the jurisdiction of a prelate, although not those things which are of the order. If, however, that power were restricted to a person, the prelate being dead, the jurisdiction would simply expire, until there was another prelate; but it does not expire, therefore it appears that this jurisdiction is more radically in the Church, than in the prelate. The Church, however, would not have had it, unless it had been delivered to her from the beginning ; for the jurisdiction of the keys is not such as are the jurisdictions which communities appoint for themselves by laws ; for since this jurisdiction is in the remission of sins, and binding, men cannot frame it for themselves ; but it is only from God, since He himself remits sins ; but in the Church there is now this jurisdiction, and in this manner, when any one is elected for a prelate, jurisdiction is conferred upon him by election, for the Church had that jurisdiction, and could not exercise it, because she was not one person ; therefore she conferred it on one man ; and then, when the chief pontiff is elected by the cardinals, he is elected by the whole Church, since they in the name of the whole Church elect ; for the whole Church cannot assemble for any election whatever ; and as the election of the whole Church confers jurisdiction, so the election of the cardinals may be so done according to the expressed will of the Church by her decrees, and constitution : but if otherwise, she confers nothing of jurisdiction, nor will he be a pontiff who has taken it upon himself. .

Whether the Church now has the power of binding and loosing.

But then any one may say, that if the power of the keys, which is in the chief pontiff, is in the Church now, the Church will have the power of binding and loosing, which is not suitable. It should be answered, that the Church received the keys from Christ, and the apostles received them as ministers of the Church ; and the Church has them now, and the prelates also, but the Church has them otherwise than the prelates ; for the Church has them in respect of origin and virtue, but the prelates have them only in respect of use. The Church is said to have the keys in respect of their virtue ; for she can confer them on a prelate by election. She is also said to have them originally ; for the power of the prelate does not take its origin from itself, but it originates from the power of the Church by election. For the Church which elected him, gives to him that jurisdiction ; but the Church receives it from no one, after she has once received it from Christ. She has them originally and virtually ; and when she confers them on a prelate, she does not confer them upon him in that manner in which she has them, to wit, not so much originally and virtually, but as to their use. . . . . But if the Church could administer the keys by herself, she would not commit them to a certain prelate. But here was the same thing ; for the jurisdiction was in the people, yet the whole people did not administer the jurisdiction, but only the appointed judges, and they commanded him to be put in ward."—*Quæs.* 48 *and* 49, *Tom.* iv., *Pt.* i., *pp.* 387, 388.

The general reader, not acquainted with patristic divinity, and especially that relating to church government, might well

ask what have I to do with this long and very wordy extract
from a Roman Catholic, and an upholder of the Papal supremacy ?
It will be seen in the second part of our answer that those who
hold the notion, that the veritable apostleship of the twelve
has been handed down by ordination to the present canonically ordained bishops, ground it chiefly on the testimony of
the fathers.   In this light the extract is of great importance.
Tostatus, in his herculean commentary, the most voluminous
ever published, displays his profound acquaintance with
patristic learning; and living before the Reformation, and under
no restraint from Protestant opposition, he is less partial than
Roman Catholics now-a-days.   It is true he is hampered with
having had to accommodate his theory to the unreasonable assumptions of the Pope.   But we have to do with his principles
rather than with his awkward application of them ; and they
are so strong that rather than abandon them, he will out-
rageously apply them.   He speaks, however, of prelates in
general, as obtaining their jurisdiction from the laity of the
Church, and that especially concerns the present question.
The principle so elaborately laid down by Tostatus is the exact
doctrine of Augustine, who in authority and influence as a
divine, is by far the most important witness of the entire
ancient Church.   He teaches beyond all question that the
body of believers generally, and not any order of clergy, is the
original seat of all government, and from which it must emanate.
The following extracts form a specimen of his doctrine on this
point, and they are given in the order in which they stand in
his writings, and as published in the book, "Whose are the
Fathers," "Peter, named from the Rock should *figuratively
represent the Church* which is built upon this Rock, and *which
hath received the keys* of the kingdom of heaven." (*Retract,
lib.* i., *cap.* 1, *tom.* i., *p.* 15.)   "Christ therefore gave the
keys to His Church, in order that what it should loose on
earth should be loosed in heaven, and what it should bind on
earth should be bound in heaven ; that is to say, that any one
who should not believe that his sins are forgiven, in the
Church, to him they should not be forgiven ; but on the
contrary, any one who being in the bosom of the Church

should believe that his sins have been pardoned, and who being corrected should turn himself from them, by that same faith and correction he should be saved." (*De Doct. Chris. lib.* i., *c.* 18., *tom.* iii., *p.* 6.) "For not without cause among all the apostles doth Peter sustain the person of this Church Catholic; for unto this Church were the keys of the kingdom of heaven given, when they were given to Peter; and when it is said unto him, 'Lovest thou me? Feed my sheep' it is said unto all." ·(*De Agone Chris.*, *c.* 30, *tom.* iii., *p.* 292.) "'As the Father hath sent me, even so send I you, and when He had said this, He breathed on them, and said unto them, Receive ye the Holy Ghost,' &c., (John xx. 21-23.) If therefore they represented the Church, and this was said to them as if it were said to the Church itself, then the peace of the Church remits sins; and when the peace is alienated from the Church, it retains sins; not according to the will of men, but according to the will of God, and the prayers of holy spiritual men, who judge all things, but they themselves are judged of no man. For the rock retains, the rock remits; the dove retains, the dove remits." (*De Baptis. contra Dona.*, *lib.* iii., *c.* 18., *tom.* vii., *p.* 48.)· "I think I am not rash to say that there are some so in the House of God, which is said to be built on the rock, and that which is called the 'holy dove' &c., which House also has received the keys, and the power of loosing and binding. If any one despised this House when it reproved and corrected him, 'Let him be to thee,' He said, 'as a heathen man and a publican.' . . . . It is said to this House, 'Bear with one another in love, keeping the unity of the spirit in the bond of peace,' and again, 'the temple of God is holy, which temple ye are.' It consists in the good, in the faithful, in the holy servants of God, spread abroad everywhere, joined together in a spiritual unity by the communion of the same sacraments, whether they know themselves by sight, or whether they do not." (*Ibid. lib.* vii., *c.* 2., *p.* 81.) "Peter denotes the body of the good, nay, rather the body of the Church, howbeit in the good. For if in Peter there were not a sacrament, (sacred sign) the Lord would not have said to him, 'I will give unto thee the keys of the

kingdom of heaven ; whatsoever thou shalt loose on earth shall
be loosed in heaven ; and whatsoever thou shalt bind on earth
shall be bound in heaven.' If this was spoken only to Peter,
then the Church doeth it not. But if this thing is done in
the Church also, that what things are bound on earth are bound
in heaven, &c., because, when the Church excommunicates, the
person excommunicated is bound in heaven, when one is
reconciled by the Church, the person reconciled is loosed in
heaven. If, I say, this thing is done in the Church, then Peter,
what time he received the keys, denoted the Holy Church.
. . . If thou art a good man, thou belongest to the body
which Peter denotes ; thou hast Christ both in the present,
and in the future." (*Expos. in Evang. Joannis, tract.* 50,
tom. ix., *p.* 152.) " Thus fares the Church by blessed hope
in this troublesome life ; of which Church the apostle Peter,
by reason of the primacy of his apostleship, is by a figurative
generality the representative. For, as regards himself in his
proper person, by nature he is one man, by grace one Christian,
by more abundant grace one, and, withal, the chief apostle ;
but when it was said to him, ' To thee I will give the keys,
&c,' he denoted the Universal Church, which in this world, by
divers temptations, like as by rains, floods, tempests, is shaken,
and faileth not, because it is founded upon the rock from
which Peter had his name. For it is not ' a Petro petra,' but
Petrus a petra ; not from Peter hath the rock its name, but
Peter his from the Rock, just as ' Christ ' is not called from
Christian, but ' Christian ' from Christ. . . . . The
Church, therefore, which is founded in Christ, did in Peter
receive from him ' the keys of the kingdom of heaven;' that is,
the power of binding and loosing sins. For that which, in
strictness of speech, the Church is in Christ, the same by
significance is Peter in the Rock ; in which significance the
Rock means Christ, Peter the Church." (*Ibid., Tract.* 124,
p. 234.) For two other important passages see *Tract.* 121,
p. 228, also *De verbis Domini in Evang. Sermo.* xiii., *tom.*
x. *pp.* 24, 25.

This is but a small specimen of the general style in which
Augustine claims for the body of the faithful in contradistinc-

tion to its pastors, the seat of power and authority. The object he had in view by this kind of argumentation was to silence the Donatists, who made everything to depend upon the presbyter and bishop, as if they were the proprietors of the Church's blessings and not merely the dispensers of them —as lords or supreme rulers of the Church, and not merely its ministers. Augustine's reasoning is to this effect: "You proud Donatists give yourselves airs of importance, and assume to be masters, when if you properly discharge the functions of your office, you perform the same as servants. What you do in your office of bishop or presbyter you do in the name of the Church; the Church preaches by you, administers the sacraments by you, governs by you, censures, suspends, absolves, excommunicates by you. You are only the ministers of the Church, and the dispensers of its rights."

Augustine's declamation against the Donatists is to the same effect as his arguments; discoursing on the words, "Put not your trust in princes" (Psalm cxlvi. 3), he says, "Therefore in Him is salvation, for salvation is the Lord's. For another Psalm saith, 'Salvation is the Lord's, and thy blessing is upon thy people.' And without cause do men claim to themselves to give salvation. Let them give it to themselves. Reply to the proud man, Thou boastest in that thou sayest that thou givest me salvation; give it to thyself; see whether thou hast it; consider well thy frailty; thou seest that thou hast it not yet. Therefore bid me not to look for it from thee, but look thou for it with me. 'Put not your trust in princes, nor in the sons of men, in whom is no salvation.' Behold, certain princes (bishops) come forth, I know not whence, and say, I baptize, and what I give is holy: if thou receive from another, thou hast received nothing; if thou receivest from me, thou hast received something. O man! O prince! wishest thou to be among "the sons of men," and among the "princes in whom is no salvation?" Have I, therefore, salvation because thou givest? Is what thou givest thine own? Or is it true that thou givest it? Or can we say that thou givest it? So the pipe may say that it giveth water; so, too, may the gutter say that itself runs; so, too, may the usher say

that he setteth free.   In the water I regard the fountain ; in
the voice of the usher I recognise the judge.   Verily, thou
shalt not be the author of my salvation.   He shall be on whom
I can rely ; of thee I am uncertain."—(*Enarratio in Psalm*
145, *tom.* viii., p. 690.)

Again he says, " What did John not know ?   That the
power of the Lord's baptism would not pass from the Lord
to any man, whereas the minister of it would quite do so :
the power of the Lord would pass from the Lord to none,
the ministry to both good and bad.   Let not the dove
be shocked at the ministry of bad men ; let her regard the power of the Lord.   What is a bad minister to
thee where there is a good Lord ?   Why needest thou care
that the herald is ill-disposed, if the Judge be well-disposed ?
What John was taught by the dove was this.   What was he
taught ?   Let himself declare again.   ' The same said to me,'
saith he, ' Upon whom thou shalt see the spirit descending as a
dove, and abiding on him, this is he which baptiseth with the
Holy Ghost.'   Then let them not deceive thee, O Dove, these
seducers who say WE baptise.   O Dove (Church) acknowledge
what the Dove hath taught : ' This is he which baptizeth
with the Holy Ghost.   By the Dove we learn that this is He.
And dost thou think that thou art baptized by the power of
the person by whose ministry thou art baptized ?   If thou
dost, thou art not yet in the body of the Dove (Church), and
if thou art not in the body of the Dove, no marvel that thou
art devoid of simplicity.   .   .   .   If the minister (*minister*)
happens to be righteous, I reckon him with Paul, I reckon
him with Peter, with these I reckon righteous ministers.
For they that are indeed righteous ministers seek not their
own glory, for they are ministers (*ministri*) ; they re-
fuse to be accounted judges (*Judicibus*).   .   .   .   ' Howbeit, Jesus himself baptized not, but his disciples.'   He and
ye not He : He in the power (*potestate*), they in the ministry
(*ministerio*).   They, in the capacity of servants (*servitutem*),
put their hand to the work of baptizing ; the power of baptizing was in Christ, and there remained."   Continuing the same
subject in a second discourse he remarks, " Christ should in

such wise do this, as to retain to Himself the power, and to none of His ministers transfer the same, this is what he learnt by the dove. For through this power, which Christ retained exclusively to Himself, and made over to none of His ministers, albeit He vouchsafed to use the service of His ministers in baptising, through this subsists the unity of the Church, which is signified by the dove, of which it is said, 'My dove is one, the only one of her mother.' For if, as I have already said, my brethren, the power were transferred from the Lord to the minister, there would be as many baptisms as ministers, and the unity of baptism would at once cease."—(*Expos. in Evang. Tract.* v. vi., *tom.* ix., pp, 18, 19, 22.)

Augustine yet further rebukes the Donatists, and all others who claim plenary powers as lords in the Church in showing that they are but servants not only to Christ, but also to the body of the faithful, and that it is not they which do this or that, but rather the church of which they are the ministers, He says, " The good Physician not only cured the sick then present, but provided also for them who were to be hereafter. There were to be men in after times, who should say, 'It is I who forgive sins, I who justify, I who sanctify, I who cure whomsoever I baptize.' Of this number are they who say, 'Touch me not.' So then in that they say, 'Touch me not,' for I am clean, they are like to that Pharisee, who had invited the Lord, and who thought that He did not know the woman, simply because He did not hinder her from touching His feet. But in another respect the Pharisee was better, because whereas he supposed Christ to be but a man, he did not believe that by a man sins could be forgiven. There was shown then a better understanding in Jews than heretics. What said the Jews ? Who is this that forgiveth sins also ? Does any man dare to usurp this to himself ? What on the other hand says the heretic ? It is I who forgive, I cleanse, I sanctify. Let not me, but Christ, answer him : O man, when I was thought by the Jews to be but a man, I forgave sins to faith. (It is not I but Christ who answereth thee.) And thou, O heretic, mere man as thou art, dost say, come, O woman, I will make thee whole. Whereas when I was thought to be but a man, I said, 'Go

woman, thy faith hath made thee whole.' They answer,
'knowing not,' as the Apostle says, 'either what they speak, or
whereof they affirm ; they answer and say, if men do not
forgive sins, then that is false which Christ saith, ' Whatsoever
ye shall loose on earth, shall be loosed in heaven also.' But
thou dost not know why this is said, and in what sense
this is said.   The Lord was about to give men the Holy Spirit,
and He wished it to be understood that sins are forgiven to
His faithful, by His Holy Spirit, and not by men's deserts.
For what art thou, O man, but an invalid who hast need of
healing.   Wouldest thou make thyself my physician ?
Together with me, seek the physician. For that the Lord might
show this more plainly, that sins are forgiven by the Holy
Spirit, which He hath given to His faithful ones, and not by
men's deserts, after He had risen from the dead, He saith in
a certain place, ' Receive ye the Holy Ghost ;" and when He
had said, ' Receive ye the Holy Ghost, He subjoined immediately, ' Whosoever sins ye remit, they are remitted unto them,
that is, the Spirit remits them, not ye.   Now the Spirit is
God.   God therefore remits, not ye.   But what are ye in
regard to the Spirit ?   ' Know ye not that ye are the temple of
God, and the Spirit of God dwelleth in you ?'   And again,
' Know ye not that your bodies are the temples of the Holy
Ghost which is in you, which ye have of God ? '   So then God
dwelleth in His holy temple, that is, in His holy faithful ones,
in His Church : by them doth He remit sins, because they
are living temples." (*Hom.* xxiii., *tom.* x., *p.* 171.)   Here
we find the most certain confirmation of the doctrine laid down
by Tostatus, viz. that the keys, the power, discipline, and
government of the Church, are given to the whole body of
believers, and that to it they originally and actually belong,
and bishops and presbyters exercise them only ministerially
not only in relation to Christ the Head, but also in relation to
the Church the body.   In these instances, and many places
elsewhere, Augustine, beyond all question, teaches that to the
body of the faithful, and not to the body of pastors, is to be
referred all the efficacy and force of the actions of the ministry,
and all the power of the keys.

It should be borne in mind that it is of no consequence to our argument whether this principle so distinctly enunciated and maintained by Augustine is in itself correct or incorrect. At present, our appeal is to the opinions and practices of the early Church, and Augustine, universally admitted to be by far its greatest authority, as a witness in such things, employs such arguments and declamation against the Donatists as to show how oblivious he must have been of any class of rulers in the Church possessing "plenary powers," or "exercising a princely regency." If there were any Church rulers in his day who pretended to have the "plenary powers" of an apostle of the twelve, they were found only among the Donatists, whom, as we have seen, Augustine in no measured terms denounced as heretics, and they have always been considered by the Catholic Church as schismatics.

We have seen how accurately Tostatus represented the sentiments of the greatest authority of the early Latin Church, in regard to the body of the faithful being the depository of all power and authority, and not the ministry, nor any portion of it. But Tostatus has also maintained very expressly that the body of the faithful who by right, and permanent inheritance, possess all power; also confer it upon their ministers, especially the highest order of them, as we should naturally infer. It will be seen that Augustine's testimony on this point is equally explicit, with this difference, however, in the place of sentiments uttered under the influence of a fierce controversy, we shall have quiet matter-of-fact statements.

In applying a portion of the 45th Psalm to the Church of Christ, on the words "Instead of thy fathers, sons have been born to thee" (v., 16), he remarks, "It was the Apostles begat thee : they were sent; they were the preachers; they are the 'Fathers.' But was it possible for them to be with us in the body for ever ? Is the Church then left desolate by their departure ? God forbid ! 'Instead of thy fathers, sons have been born to thee.' . . . Instead of the Apostles, sons have been born to thee; bishops have been appointed. For in the present day, whence do the bishops throughout all the world derive their origin ? The Church itself calls them

Fathers ; the Church itself brought them forth, and placed them on the seats of the Fathers. Think not thyself abandoned, then, because thou seest not Peter, nor seest Paul, seest not those through whom thou wast born. Out of thine offspring has a body of Fathers been raised up to thee." How very different is the pedigree claimed for a bishop by Augustine, compared with that claimed for him by modern high Anglicans. The modern pedigree, as made out by Dr Wordsworth, the present Bishop of Lincoln, and the proposer to convocation of the question under examination, well represents the young but vigorous school of high Anglicanism. It is as follows : "The succession of the chief pastors to the Apostles has been directly *authorised* by Christ, . . . as follows : Christ being sent by the Father (Heb. iii. 1 ; 1 Peter ii. 25) to be the great Apostle, Bishop, and Pastor of the Church, as He is called in Scripture, and being visibly consecrated to that office by the Holy Ghost, sent His Apostles as His Father sent Him (Acts x. 38 ; Luke iii. 22). He gave to them the Holy Ghost as His Father had given to Him (John xx. 21, 22 ; xvii. 18) ; and commissioned them to execute the same apostolic, episcopal, and pastoral office, in their own persons and in that of their successors, for the governing of His Church (2 Tim. ii. 2) until His coming again, promising to be with them alway, even unto the end of of the world." (*Theoph. Ang.*, pp. 97, 98.) How contrary is all this to what we have learnt from Augustine, and what we have just seen respecting his modest but glowing account of the making of bishops. We are told distinctly that the Apostles constituted the Church, but that they could only be with the Church as long as they lived. Were then God's faithful people "left desolate by their departure ?" No ; bishops were found in all parts of the world ; but whence did they "derive their origin ?" "The Church itself brought them forth (constituted them), and placed them on the seats of the Fathers," that is, the Apostles. Look at this pedigree and look at that ; compare the ancient account of constituting bishops with the modern one—the teaching of the fourth with that of the nineteenth century. The contrast could not well be greater. Augustine speaks of bishops being "placed on the seats of the Fathers." Bishops in his day were believed to be presiding in Churches in certain cities, either founded by the Apostles, or while they lived; but the Church in which Augustine presided in the village of Hippo had no such pretensions. Tertullian enumerated in his day several cities that had, or were thought to have had, such seats. The city of Alexandria was one respecting which Jerome says, "For at Alexandria also, from Mark the Evangelist to the bishops Hereclas and Dionisius, the presbyters always called one elected from among themselves, and placed in a higher rank, bishop; just as an army may constitute its general, or deacons may elect one of themselves, whom they know to be diligent, and call him archdeacon." (*Ad Evagrium, tom.* ii., p. 329.) These bishops mentioned by name, as well as their predecessors for about 200 years, were real successors of the Apostles, living in a city, and presiding in a Church in that city, if not founded by one of the twelve, yet founded by one of their immediate disciples, but without any pretensions to the apostleship of the twelve, nor did the very learned Jerome pretend it for them. The fact is, we have no such pretensions recorded during the first four or five centuries of the Church. We shall find, as Bishop Pearson says in his exposition of the Creed, "the Apostles," that is, the twelve, "are continued unto us only in their writings." Bishop Wordsworth seems to make Christ Himself an apostle among His servants the twelve Apostles, only placing Him first in the line of succession, but claiming for the twelve the SAME *Apostolic, Episcopal,* and *Pastoral* office with which He Himself had been entrusted by the Father, and not only claiming it for them in their own persons, but also "in that of their successors." So that God's sending, Christ's sending, and the Apostles' sending, are not represented as descending, but as equal, grades of sending; whereas Clement, "whose name is in the book of life," and whose epistle is the most ancient, authentic, and valuable of all the apostolical records, represents the several sendings as of descending grades. All the grades of sending are gone through, and coming to the last and lowest, he says,

B

"The Apostles appointed their first-fruits, having proved them by the Spirit, for bishops and deacons." Tertullian also goes through these grades of sending; but he is so far from considering a bishop to have the same Apostolic, Episcopal, and Pastoral office as that of Christ, or one of the twelve, that he merges him among his flock. His words are, "That which the Churches (not the bishops exclusively) have received from the Apostles, the Apostles from Christ, Christ from God."

Firmilian, who lived in the middle of the third century, about fifty years after Tertullian, gives substantially the same account and maintains the same teaching as Augustine and his imitator Tostatus, viz., that all power is lodged in the body of the faithful. He says, "The power of remitting sins was given to the apostles, and to the churches which they founded, and to the bishops who succeeded to the apostles by a vicarious ordination." Again he states, "All power and grace is placed in the Church where the presbyters preside."—(*Opera Cypri. Epist.* 75, *tom.* ii., pp. 221, 225.)

Firmilian, like his friend Cyprian, fully recognised "the majesty of the people." But here it must be confessed that there is something very much like modern high Anglicanism. "Bishops who succeeded the apostles by a vicarious ordination." This is a Cyprianic phrase to which we shall have to recur presently, when it will be found that the ordination or creating of a bishop is chiefly effected by the laity, and that he is considered to be a successor not to the kind of office and power belonging to the twelve apostles, but to the office and power ascribed to the seventy disciples, whom all the Fathers commonly called apostles.

We must now come back to Augustine, and shew that in his application of a portion of the 45th Psalm to the chief rulers of the Church in his day, he did what was commonly done by his brethren of the early Latin Church. Thus, in the excellent Commentary on the Psalms, commonly ascribed to Jerome, we read, "O Church, apostles have been thy fathers, because they begat thee. But now, since they have departed from the world, thou hast in their stead sons—bishops which have been created by thee."—(*Tom.* viii., p. 68). Here most certainly we are taught that the apostles constituted the Church, but the Church created the bishops.

The learned Ruffinus, a little earlier than Augustine, gives the same account, with this difference, he defines what kind of rulers he understands. "Princes," that is, "masters and teachers (*magistros et doctores.*)"—(*Tom.* ii., f. 104). The phrase, "masters and teachers," is a citation from the Latin version of the New Testament as it stood in his day. Now the citation itself shews beyond a doubt that he did not consider the apostolic office of the Twelve to be perpetuated in his time by any class of rulers in the Church ; if he did, why did he pass over the first part and quote the latter of the following text ? "And he gave some, apostles ; and some, prophets; and some, evangelists; and some, *masters and teachers.*"—(*Eph.* iv. 11.) This learned presbyter, by "masters and teachers," included presbyters as well as bishops, who, he maintains, had been created by the Church.

Chrysostom, a Greek Father, on the words of the Psalm under consideration expatiates very eloquently, but like Gregory the Great, and other Fathers, considers the apostles to have been succeeded by their writings, or rather as still ruling by them. He says, " The apostles traversed the whole world, became rulers more lordly than all rulers, than kings more mighty. For kings, indeed, exercise power whilst they live, but when they die their power lapses ; but these, when dead, rule the more. The laws of kings have force within their own dominions, but the ordinances of the fishermen have been extended everywhere through the habitable earth. The Emperor of the Romans cannot legislate for the Persians, nor can the King of the Persians for the Romans; but these men of Palestine have imposed their laws alike on Romans and Persians, Thracians and Scythians, Indians and Moors. Nay, all over the world, not only while living have they thus been powerful but also since they were dead ; and of those by whom these laws have been received there is not one who would not a thousand times rather lose his life than revolt against them."—(*Expos. in Psalm* xliv., *tom.* v., p. 181.)

From the theory, or doctrine of the power and authority of

the body of the faithful, called the Church, we pass to what was her practice as well as doctrine.   Clement of Rome, the most valuable of the apostolic fathers, writing " to the Church dwelling at Corinth," says, " We are of opinion there-fore that those appointed by the apostles, or afterwards by other eminent men, with the consent of the whole Church, &c., cannot be justly dismissed from the ministry.   For our sin will not be small, if we eject from the episcopate those who have blamelessly and holily fulfilled its duties.   Blessed are those presbyters who, having finished their course before now   .   .   .   .   for they have no fear, lest any one deprive them of the place now appointed for them.   But we see that ye have removed some men of excellent behaviour from the ministry."   (Ch. xliv.)

Here Clement shows that the rulers in "the Church, dwelling at Corinth," had been appointed by the consent of the whole Church, and that the Church had power, and made use of it, is too obvious to need any remark.   The question is, did it of right belong to them ?   We conclude it did, or Clement must have said something more than merely entreat them to make a more Christian-like use of it.

But Cyprian is the great authority on this subject ; we shall therefore at once confer with him.   Having been con-sulted by some Christian people in Spain, respecting two unworthy bishops, he with about forty of his brethren, sent a joint letter to these Christian people in trouble, respecting their chief rulers, in which this plain and definite principle is laid down, viz., " that the people themselves have the power, either of choosing worthy priests, or of rejecting unworthy ones."   The people had, in fact, exercised this power in rejecting two bishops, and choosing other two in their places. These rejected bishops had given their own account of the matter to Stephen, bishop of Rome, and the result was that they were determined to retain their office, but two others had been appointed in their places, and what are the people and clergy to do ?   In their emergency they consult Cyprian, bishop of Carthage, at that time in no respect second to the bishop of Rome.   Such then is the origin of this synodical

letter.   Now what are its chief contents?   Such as here
follow.   "Nor let the people flatter themselves, that they can
be free from the contagion of sin, while communicating with a
priest who is a sinner, and yielding their consent to the unjust
and unlawful episcopacy of their overseer, when the divine
reproof by Hosea the prophet threatens, and says: 'Their
sacrifices shall be as the bread of mourning; all that eat
thereof shall be polluted;' teaching manifestly, and showing
that all are absolutely bound to the sin who have been con-
taminated by the sacrifice of a profane and unrighteous priest;
which, moreover, we find to be manifested also in Numbers,
when Korah, and Dathan, and Abiram claimed for themselves
the power of sacrificing in opposition to Aaron the priest.
There also the Lord commanded by Moses that the people
should be separated from them, lest, being associated with the
wicked, themselves also should be bound closely in the same
wickedness.   'Separate yourselves,' said He, 'from the tents
of these wicked and hardened men, and touch not those things
which belong to them, lest ye perish together in their sins.'
On which account a people obedient to the Lord's precepts, and
fearing God, ought to separate themselves from a sinful prelate,
and   not   to   associate   themselves   with   the   sacrifices of a
sacrilegious priest, especially since they themselves have the
power either of choosing worthy priests, or of rejecting
unworthy ones.   Which very thing, too, we observe to come
from divine authority, that the priest should be chosen in the
presence of the people under the eyes of all, and should be
approved worthy, and suitable by public judgment and testimony.   .   .   .   .   And this was subsequently observed, according to divine instruction, in the Acts of the Apostles, when
Peter speaks to the people of ordaining an apostle in the
place of Judas.   'Peter,' it says, 'stood up in the midst of
the disciples, and the multitude were in one place.'   Neither
do we observe that this was regarded by the apostles only in
the ordination of bishops and priests, but also in those of
deacons, of which matter itself, also it is written in their
Acts, vi. 2.   (*Epist.* 67., *tom.* ii., *pp.* 171, 172.

Here we certainly learn that, in the opinion of Cyprian,

the believing laity had the chief, if not plenary power in making and unmaking bishops. The reasons of his belief in no respect affect our argument. But other Christian fathers made use of the two instances in the Acts of the Apostles in a similar way. Thus Chrysostom referring to the appointment of the seven deacons remarks, "the apostles themselves might indeed have made the election, as moved by the Spirit : but nevertheless, they desire the testimony of the people. But, the choice of the men, they make over to the people, that they might not seem to act from favour : just as God also leaves it to Moses to choose as elders those whom he knew." (*Expos. Acta Apost. hom.* iii., *tom.* ix., *p.* 26.) Again, he observes, " For when the apostles ordained the seven, they made it common to the people, and when Peter [ordained] Matthias, [he made it common] to all that were then present, both men and women." (*Expos. in Epist. ad. Cor.* II., *hom.* xviii., *tom.* x., 569.)

But we must not at present leave Cyprian, who, on the question under consideration, is the most important ancient witness which can be adduced, and whose testimony with modern high Anglicans should be final ; for Dr Pusey, their Corypheus, considered " Christian prophecy as having been vouchsafed to St. Cyprian, along the whole course of his episcopate." (*On Daniel, p.* 627.) He further remarks that Cyprian was " guided by revelations along the whole course of an anxious episcopate ; " that he had had " abundant revelations," some of which are enumerated, and to which is added, " that He whose ' witness ' he was, bore witness to him, after death; that he was seen thrice since, in glory ; once, as one to whom it had been ' given to sit down on the throne ' of the judge ; and people might well shrink from judging for themselves of his words, by whom living the Holy Spirit spake, and who is now an assessor of their judge." (*Preface to the Translation of Cyprian's Epistles, pp.* xxi-xxii.)

Now, through what human medium did Cyprian consider that bishops were made ? And how did he consider that he was made ? As most things are more striking and impressive when viewed in contrast, we shall first state the peculiar but high Anglo-catholic theory of making bishops known chiefly in the latter half of the nineteenth century, and then contrast with it the common Africo-catholic theory of making bishops in the third century. The present Bishop of Lincoln, in his catechism of peculiar but high Anglo-catholicism, called by the name of "Theophilus Anglicanus," asks, "Are the bishops of the Church of England *made* by the sovereign?" and answers, "No; no *earthly* power can *make* a bishop. Kings do not *make*, but only do *place* bishops. Consecration *makes* a bishop; the *Royal grant places* him. His *beneficium* is *a Rege*, but his *officium is a Deo*. His *commission* is from Christ, his *permission* to *exercise* it in special *places*, and over special *persons*, is from the *Prince*."—Pp. 331, 332. To shew that no earthly power can make a bishop, and to point out how he is made, he supplies "the young student" with the following reason:—"The English *Ordinal* is entitled 'The form and manner of *making*, &c., of *bishops*,' &c." Now nowhere in the Ordinal are bishops said to be *made*. Deacons are said to be *made*, but priests ordered, and bishops consecrated. We cannot but notice, in passing, that as a matter of fact, kings, or rather the supreme powers in this realm, do make bishops, as well as place them. Beyond all question, the supreme powers determined that Dr Temple should be the Bishop of the see of Exeter, and no other man. We shall see presently that the power, whatever it was, that fixed the man for the office of bishop was considered to make him. We believe the ministerial office is one instituted of God, and the man who rightly receives the office may be said to be made of God, and no doubt Bishop Wordsworth referred to the Ordinal in this point of view; but it should be observed, consecrating a bishop is not making a bishop, and if the bishops had the right of fixing on the person to be consecrated, as well as consecrating him, then they might be considered to make him, but not according to primitive antiquity; for those over whom he had to preside were considered to have the right of electing him, and in fact were considered to be his makers. The modern doctrine of High Anglicanism is, that bishops make bishops, and if this is canonically done, Christ may be said to make them. The ancient doctrine of the Catholic Church is, that the laity and clergy over whom the bishop is to preside make him, and if this is properly performed, then Christ is considered to have made him. Again, one teaches that Christ makes bishops by bishops conferring on the candidate a "perfect and unbroken transmission of the original ministerial commission," the other that Christ makes bishops by their being duly elected to the office of His appointment by those over whom the bishop is to preside. In the former case, the bishops who duly perform their part are considered to be the vicars of Christ, and the appointment is considered to be Christ's; in the latter case, if the laity and clergy properly perform their part, they are considered to act in the place of Christ, and the act is regarded as His. In the one case the bishop thus made is supposed to succeed to the peculiar apostleship of the Twelve; in the other, not to the apostleship of the Twelve, but rather to the office of the seventy disciples, whom all the fathers designate apostles, and the office of these they considered to be perpetuated, but not that of the Twelve.

An examination of a brief statement of Cyprian in relation to these points will form a basis for the discussion of these questions. He says, "Nor do I boast of these things, but bring them forth with sorrow, since you set yourself up as a judge of God and Christ, who says to the Apostles, and thereby to all rulers (*præpositis*), who by a vicarious ordination are successors of the Apostles, 'He that heareth you heareth me; and he that despiseth you despiseth me, and he that despiseth me despiseth Him that sent me.'" (Luke x. 16.) On this we shall raise the following questions. When was the office of these rulers instituted? Who were these rulers? How were they appointed to their office? And who are the Apostles of whom they are said to be the successors? Here it is purposed to point out what Cyprian taught on these points in the middle of the third century, and what is now taught in this latter half of the nineteenth century by high Anglicans.

When was the office of these rulers instituted? Obviously when Christ appointed the seventy disciples. This is what Cyprian teaches, and we gather from his language that the office is of permanent institution, and that those who appoint to it act in the place of Christ. Cyprian and the fathers generally consider that when Christ appointed the seventy disciples whom they all call apostles, he instituted the office of the Christian ministry to be perpetuated to the end of the Gospel dispensation. But supposing these ancient men are all wrong, that does not affect our argument ; we are concerned with their opinions, not with their reasons for them. The fathers commonly symbolized the twelve fountains of Elim with the twelve Apostles. As these fountains were not replaced, so neither did they consider that the twelve Apostles could be replaced. The seventy palm-trees they symbolized with a class of ministers that required to be replaced, but who derived all their virtues from the fountains, the twelve Apostles. So taught Tertullian, Origen, Gregory of Nyssa, Ambrose, Theophylact, Aquinas, and Cyril of Alexandria, from whom we may learn substantially the sentiments of the others, who, as cited by Aquinas in his *Catena Aurea*, says, " In the Book of Numbers, also, it is written of the children of Israel that they came to Elim, which is, by interpretation, 'ascent,' and there were twelve fountains of water, and seventy palm-trees. For when we fly to spiritual refreshment we shall find twelve fountains, namely, the holy Apostles, from whom we imbibe the knowledge of salvation as from the well-springs of the Saviour ; and seventy palms, that is, those who are *now* (*nunc*) appointed by Christ." (*On Luke* x. 1.)

Cyprian certainly here, in his judgment, is referring to the institution of the ministerial office as done once for all, as doubtless it was instituted in the apostolic age. But according to the present high Anglican notion, the office is instituted every time a person is appointed to it. This appears to be the doctrine of Bishop Wordsworth at page 16, and again, at page 23, he seems to teach that consecration makes a bishop by conferring on him the office from God, rather than consecrating him to the office instituted by God. This high Anglican theory of making a bishop is a new thing in the earth, and nobody knows exactly what it is. Dean Hook considers that at consecration is conferred " a perfect and unbroken transmission of the original ministerial commission." How a bishop is made, and how the Pope is made, is plain enough, as taught by Tostatus and given above (pp. 5-7), but not a word is said about any mysterious or incomprehensible influence wandering along fourteen centuries, through clean, and some exceedingly unclean creatures, through some saints, and not a few consecrated monsters. It does not appear that, with all the outrageous assumptions of the Papists, and their unaccountable beliefs, they have any such carnal notion of apostolical succession as, alas! is but too common to high Anglicans of the present day. The *theory* of apostolical succession, as held by Roman Catholics, is both intelligible and rational. When the Pope dies there is an interregnum of the supposed apostolical successor, though it is maintained that the office still exists. None of the bishops of the Romish Church profess to hold the office, and cannot pretend to confer it. The cardinals, as we are told by Tostatus, elect the Pope, but in his opinion they represent the whole body of the Church, and the Church, through these cardinals, her representatives, confers the right on the object of her choice to supply the vacated office of St Peter. Is it said that Tostatus, living 400 years ago, is not an authority from whom to learn the present state of the Papacy, seeing it is ever given to change? Be it so. But we maintain that even now the present Pope, according to Roman teaching, is not considered to have received the peculiar qualifications to fit him for the supposed office fof St Peter through any human medium whatever. Thus writes a Roman Catholic authority :—"Christ in person bestowed supreme authority on St Peter, whilst his successors receive the same power from Christ also, but yet by means of a lawful election to the see of Rome." "The Roman Pontiff succeeds in apostleship . . . not by concession from any mortal, but by office, as occupying St Peter's chair." —*The Apostolical Succession Explained, &c., by a Priest of the Order of Charity*, pp. 31, 32.)

This theory and form of making a Pope is not unlike what it was in the days of Cyprian, but then "the Church dwelling at Rome" was not supposed to be everywhere else. At that time there was a "Church dwelling at Corinth," one at Carthage, where Cyprian presided, and about 700 other such places in North Africa alone, at each of which a Church dwelt, having over it a bishop or a presiding presbyter. At that time the laity of "the Church dwelling at Rome" could themselves elect a bishop without the intervention of any such officers as the cardinals. The following is an illustration of the manner of making a bishop of the Church at Rome in the time of Cyprian : " It is said Fabian had come to Rome with some others from the country, and staying there, in the most remarkable manner, by divine and celestial grace, came to the lot (was made bishop). When all the brethren had assembled in the church for the purpose of ordaining (χειροτονίας, meaning making or electing) one to succeed in the episcopate, though there were very many eminent and illustrious men in the estimation of many, Fabian being present, no one thought of any other man. They relate, further, that a dove, suddenly flying down from on high, sat upon his head, exhibiting a scene like that of the Holy Spirit descending upon our Saviour in the form of a dove. Upon this the whole body exclaimed, with all eagerness and with one voice, as if moved by the one Spirit of God, that he was worthy ; and without delay they took and placed him upon the bishop's throne."—(*Euseb. Hist. Eccles.*, lib. vi., c. 29, pp. 439, 440.)

We now proceed to answer the second question : Who were the rulers who by a vicarious ordination succeeded the apostles? By apostles, meaning of course the seventy disciples specially sent by Christ, as Cyprian shows. Undoubtedly he included bishops and presbyters, for, under the term rulers, Cyprian commonly included both. He does so in the following statement : " Whence we learn that it is not allowed to any to baptize except to rulers within the Church [*in ecclesia præpositis*], and who are appointed by the law of the gospel and the ordinance of the Lord . . . and that no one can usurp to himself, against bishops and priests [*episcopos et sacerdotes*]."

Here we are compelled to anticipate the answer to the last question, namely : Who are the apostles of whom these rulers are the successors ? Cyprian plainly teaches that rulers, including himself and bishops generally, succeed the seventy

disciples.   But what do modern high Anglicans teach on this
point, and represent Cyprian as teaching in the very sentence
under examination?   Bishop Wordsworth, who well represents
the Laudean and Tractarian school in his catechism of this
peculiar doctrine which he calls, "Instruction for the young
student," asks, * Whom do bishops succeed and represent"?
and answers: "The holy apostles;" and one fallacious reason
out of many is as follows from Cyprian: "Bishops are rulers
who succeed the apostles by a vicarious ordination."   The
"young" and ill-informed "student" would in this connection
suppose that bishops and bishops only, and such as are now in
our Church, succeed the twelve apostles.   Elsewhere· the
Bishop states, "as the Apostles are succeeded by *Bishops*
in the Church, so the *Seventy* by *Presbyters.*"   (*On Luke*
x. 1.)   Now what Cyprian really teaches is, that rulers,
whethers bishops or presbyters, succeed the seventy disciples,
not the twelve apostles.   His own statement which we
repeat is, "Christ says to the apostles, [the seventy], and
thereby to all rulers [both bishops and presbyters] who by a
vicarious ordination, are successors of the apostles, ' He that
heareth you heareth me: and he that despiseth you despiseth
me, &c."   (*Luke*, x. 16.)

We come now to the third question.   How were these
rulers, and especially Cyprian, appointed to their office.   The
answer obviously is, "by a vicarious ordination."   It remains
for us to ascertain what Cyprian intends by this phrase which
he has made sufficiently clear in his writings.   It occurs in a
letter in which he is called upon to vindicate his position as
bishop of the Church at Carthage.   A bishop and confessor in
the Decian persecution, who had taken part with Novatian,
the rival bishop to Cornelius bishop of Rome, wrote his
mind to Cyprian upon the subject of that quarrel, and in
terms of contempt, signified to him that he held him as
unworthy of his station and dignity in the Church.   He
wanted also to have a scruple removed; how any who com-
municated with Cyprian could reasonably be considered to
communicate with the Church.   To all which Cyprian returns
an answer of great severity, and all the powers of Cyprian's

former profession as a rhetorician are employed to convince his accuser and others that by the will of God he is bishop of the Church at Carthage. In this important letter not a syllable is uttered of either clergy or bishops taking any part in his ordination ; but in proof that he was made bishop by the Divine will, he argues as follows :—" You are inquiring diligently into my conduct, and, after the judgment of God who maketh bishops, are desirous of judging, I say not me (for of what account am I ?), but of the judgment of God and of Christ. This is not to believe in God, this is to be a rebel against Christ and against His Gospel, that whereas He says, 'Are not two sparrows sold for a farthing? yet neither of them falls to the ground without the will of the Father,' and His majesty and truth prove that even the smallest things do not come to pass without the cognizance and permission of God, you suppose that the priests of God are, without His cognizance, ordained in the Church ?" (*Epist.* 66.) Here we shall find that in his customary manner he is referring to his ordination as an act of Divine Providence.

Fortunatus was ordained a rival bishop to Cyprian at Carthage. Now what was Cyprian to do, placed as he was in this position ? The only tribunal to which an appeal could be made at that early stage of the Church was the common opinion of the faithful. As Cyprian had used the utmost powers of his rhetoric to defend Cornelius, Bishop of Rome, against Novatian, his rival, he now in an eloquent letter asks the sympathy and support of the bishop, clergy, and people of the Church dwelling at Rome, and here again in his best style vindicates the Divine right to his position as bishop signified by the will of the people, and their will only. But he shall speak for himself, as recorded in his letter to his brethren at Rome. " No one, pleasing himself and swelling with pride, would found a new heresy separate and apart, unless any be of such sacrilegious temerity and of so abandoned mind, as to think that a priest is made without the judgment of God, whereas the Lord says in His Gospel, 'Are not two sparrows sold for a farthing? and one of them does not fall on the ground without the will of your Father.' When he saith that

not even the least things are done without the will of God,
does any one think that the very highest and chief things are
done in the Church without either God's knowledge or permission ? and that priests, that is, His stewards, are not
ordained by His appointment ?   This is not to have that ·
faith by which we live ; this is not to give honour to God,
by whose will and arbitrement we know and believe that all
things are ruled and governed.   In truth, there are bishops
not made by the will of God, but such as are made out
of the Church, such as are made against the order and
tradition of the Gospel, as the Lord Himself in the twelve '
prophets lays it down, and says, ' They have set up kings, but
not by me.'   . . .   But (I speak on provocation, I speak
in sorrow, I speak on compulsion) when a bishop is put in the
place of one deceased, when in time of peace he is chosen by
the suffrages of the whole people, when in persecution he is
protected by the aid of God, faithfully united to all his colleagues, approved by his own people in the exercise of his
episcopate for now four years. . . . .   After all this,
they yet, in addition, having had a pseudo-bishop ordained
for them by heretics, dare to set sail, and to carry letters from
schismatic and profane persons to the chair of Peter, &c.   .
. . In the dignity of the Catholic Church, dearest brother,
is the faithful and uncorrupt majesty of the people placed
within it?   Is the episcopal authority and power also to be
therefore laid aside, that those who are set without the Church
may say they wish to judge a ruler in the Church ? heretics,
a Christian ? wounded, the sound ? &c. . . .   Now, though
I am aware, dearest brother, that, by reason of the mutual
love which we owe and manifest towards each other, you
always read my epistles to the very eminent clergy who there
preside with you, and to your most holy and flourishing people,
yet now I both exhort and beg of you, to do at my request,
what on other occasions you do of your own accord and of
courtesy, and read this my epistle, that so, if any contagion of
poisoned language or pestilent reports has crept in amongst
the brethren, it may be wholly removed from their ears and
hearts." (*Epist.* 59.)

، Cyprian distinctly maintains that the ordination which he calls vicarious, and by which he was made a successor of the apostles, was in his case effected by the people and the people only. Elsewhere he calls the suffrages of the people divine, inasmuch as they were indicative of the divine will. Writing to the whole people, he states, "Certain presbyters, mindful of their old conspiracy, and retaining their ancient venom against my episcopate, yea against *your suffrage* and the sanction of God, renew their old attack upon us, and with their wonted treachery again resume their unholy machinations. : '. . They have from their own consciences passed sentence upon themselves ; in accordance with your divine suffrages (*vestra divina suffragia*) * the conspirators and wicked men have voluntarily expelled themselves from the Church. . . . My tears flowing by day and night, that *the priest whom you made* with so great love and zeal is not allowed even yet to greet you, not even yet to throw himself into your embrace." (*Epist.* 43). Cyprian does not give us the remotest hint that he received the apostleship of the twelve through a line of bishops from the apostles, but teaches that he was made a successor to the office of the seventy apostles, as he and the fathers generally called them. It must be admitted, however, that the case of Cyprian is rather an exceptional one, for, according to his own account of other ordinations, with the consent of the people is generally associated the consent of the clergy, particularly of the presbyters, and also of the neighbouring bishops. Thus, speaking with approval of the ordination of Cornelius, Bishop of Rome, he says, "He was made bishop by very many (sixteen) of our colleagues then present in the city of Rome, who sent to us letters, touching his ordination, remarkable for their high and honourable testimony and praise. Cornelius, moreover, was made bishop by the sanction of God and his Christ, by the testimony of almost

---

* In the translation of Cyprian's epistles, of which Dr Pusey is one of the editors, we have "your and the Divine suffrages." About a dozen editions have been examined, and in only one of them do we find "*vestra et divina suffragia.*" This different reading does not materially alter the sense, as with Cyprian the suffrages of the people were considered to be the expression of the Divine will.

all the clergy, by the suffrage of the people who were then present, and by the college of ancient priests and good men; at a time when no one had been made before him, when the place of Fabian, that is, when the place of Peter and the rank of the sacerdotal chair, was vacant." (*Epist.* 59.) In the case of the ordination of Cyprian, five out of eight presbyters who voted were against him; consequently he makes no mention of the clergy in connection with his own ordination. But such was "the majesty of the people" in his estimation, that they alone, without the consent of the clergy, were a sufficient indication of the Divine will, and by them he considered himself to have received a vicarious ordination, as if performed by Christ himself.

Pontius, a deacon of Cyprian, in recording the life and sufferings of his bishop in relation to his ordination, says, "For the proof of his good works, I think that this one thing is enough, that by the judgment of God and the favour of the people, he was chosen to the office of the priesthood and the degree of the episcopate while still a neophyte, and, as it was considered, a novice."

Many years after the time of Cyprian, good men believed that the free and unconstrained election of the believing laity was regarded as expressive of the will of God. So Remigius, an archbishop who flourished about A. D. 470, both believed and taught. As this good man has given substantially what the fathers have taught, from Origen down to his own times, respecting the nature and kinds of apostles, and that the reader may know among what class of apostles to put such ministers as Cyprian, and see what an amazing difference there is between the ancient theory of apostleship and the theory of high Anglicans of the nineteenth century, we shall give a lengthy extract from him, from which it will be seen how the ancients discriminated in regard to the various kinds of senders, and those sent, in comparison of high Anglicans of the present century, who make no such discrimination, but regard all who send and all who are sent after a particular canonical form, of whatever character each may be, alike successors of the twelve Apostles.

On Romans i. 1, Remigius, citing the word "an Apostle," remarks upon it as follows :—" This is a Greek term ; in Latin it is interpreted ' sent.' He heard of the Lord, ' I *will send* thee far off to the Gentiles.' But of apostles there are four kinds : the first is that which is not made of men, neither by man, but of God only, of the number of whom were Moses, Isaiah, and many others of the prophets, and the twelve Apostles, because, although they *were sent* by the man Christ, yet He was both man and true God. Therefore it was said to Moses, ' I *will send* thee to Pharaoh ;' also to Isaiah, ' whom *shall I send*, and who will go for us ?' . . . A second kind which is of God, but by man ; of the number of whom is Joshua, who by the command and will of God *was sent* by Moses. Very many others also have been chosen for the merits of their life by the election of the people and the will of God. For the will of the people is for the most part the will of God. A third kind, which is of man only, and not of God. When any one is chosen by the favour of men, not for their good conduct, nor for the cause of religion, but for the relationship to the nobility ; or is chosen to the honour of a priest for a reward ; of the number of whom are such as those described by the blessed Ambrose, who says, ' O bishop! unless thou hadst given a hundred golden coins, thou wouldest not have been a bishop to-day.' Of the number of these are those also of whom it is said in the Book of Kings, who lived in the times of Jeroboam, ' They filled their hands (were consecrated) that they might become the priests of idols.' Of these and such like the Lord says by the prophet, ' They have reigned, but not by me ; they have been princes, and I knew not.' (Hosea viii. 4.) There is also a fourth kind of apostles, which is neither of God nor by man, but is constituted of itself only, as are false prophets and false apostles, saying, ' The Lord saith,' whereas the Lord hath not sent them.' (*In Epist. ad Rom. Bibl. Mag. Vet. Patr.*, tom. v., pt. iii., pp. 809, 810.)

We have seen how Cyprian regarded himself as a minister of Christ, and by what human instrumentality. He considered himself to be a successor to the office of the seventy apostles,

C

but not of any one pretending to hold the office, or assuming
to confer it, for the people could have no such pretensions.
It is plain, also, in this extract from Remigius, which we can
vouch to be the doctrine of the fathers from Origen down to
his time, in what sense he considered ministers to be apostles
of Christ, and through what medium. The only human
medium he thought of most importance to notice, through
which the minister obtained his commission, was the free
election of the laity. May we not be absolutely certain that
he knew nothing whatever of the modern high Anglican theory
of apostles making apostles by conferring the apostleship of
the Twelve ?

Bishop Wordsworth, as we have seen, maintains, by a most
unwarrantable application of the language of Cyprian, that
our bishops succeed the Twelve by a vicarious ordination.
But what can the bishop mean by the phrase on his theory of
sending apostles ? He states that Christ " sent His apostles
as His Father had sent Him, ...   and commissioned
them to execute the same apostolic, episcopal, and pastoral
office in their own persons and in that of their successors."
In this mode of sending, the very idea of a vicarious ordination is inadmissible, for Christ as mediator, to whom all power
was given in heaven and on earth, performed no vicarious
ordination in appointing the Twelve ; no more did they in
appointing their successors, if the bishop's theory of sending
is correct. The papal theory of apostolic succession, in form
at least, is tolerable ; but this is intolerable. The papal
system admits but of one pretender at a time to the apostleship of the Twelve ; the modern high Anglican theory admits
of an indefinite number of such pretenders. The papal system
teaches that the pretended receiver of the apostolic office
derives it through no human medium whatever ; the modern
high Anglican theory maintains that it is derived by ordination through a precarious line of men, some good, some indifferent, some monsters in human form, till you get to Christ
Himself and God the Father, from whom the apostleship first
proceeded. Bishop Wordsworth, with high Anglicans in
general, consider that the apostolic office comes from Christ to

the present bishops of our Church through the Roman popes, each of whom, it is admitted, possessed it. In his little book, "Union with Rome," in which he maintains that "the Church of Rome is the Apocalyptic Babylon," by way of allaying the fears of some of his high Anglican brethren, lest by such an admission they should feel themselves to be cut off from all revealed means of salvation, he comforts them by the consideration that "the validity of the commission is not impaired by the unworthiness of those *through* whom it was conveyed." (P. 75.) Now, what is the validity of the commission on which, according to high Anglicans of modern times, the hopes of heaven and eternal happiness are made to depend ? That the apostleship of the Twelve is now possessed by the bishops of the Church of England, but for which her members in the sight of Christ would be out of the pale of the true Church, without sacraments and the appointed means of grace. Oh, what a simpleton that man must be who rests his hopes upon a thing that is more uncertain than a delusive dream ! These high Anglicans all hold fast by the chair of Peter, by the see of Rome. It is not pretended that the apostleship comes through any other channel. Now, let us see how it is supposed to come in this way. The Lord Jesus Christ conferred the apostleship on St Peter. Now this is certain, and as true as the Gospel. Peter at Rome (if ever he were there, which is thought by able and sober-minded men to be extremely doubtful in point of fact) did confer, according to Tertullian, Ruffinus, and others, the apostleship on Presbyter Clement ; or rather, if these good men were wrong, according to Irenæus and Eusebius, did confer the apostleship on Anacletus ; or rather, if these were all wrong, according to Damasus and Augustine, did confer the Apostleship on Linus. Before we can start from Rome with the apostleship of Peter, it will be necessary to indulge in a series of suppositions. We must suppose that he did confer his own apostleship upon some one of the men whose names follow—Linus, Clement, Anacletus, Cletus—taking it for granted that they were all real persons, not one of them a myth, and leaving the order of their succession a profound mystery. Overlooking the fact, admitted

by high Anglicans, that we have no evidence in Holy Scripture of the apostleship of the Twelve being transferred to any
one, let us suppose that this doctrine, contrary to our Sixth
Article, is required, though not contained in Scripture, and
cannot be proved thereby, yet nevertheless is to be believed as
an article of the faith, and be thought requisite and necessary
to salvation.   Let us also suppose, directly contrary to the
express teaching of Augustine and Tostatus, a Roman Catholic
divine of great learning, that Peter gave the keys to his successor, and that so they were handed down from successor to
successor, and that Peter did not give them to the Church,
nor the Church to Peter's successor when the chair was vacant.
With these and sundry other suppositions we are now prepared to depart from Rome, with the supposed apostleship of
Peter coming down the supposed apostolic line (for even now
we must still keep supposing) to the Reformation.   But from
this time the transfer of the supposed apostleship of Peter, or
any one of the Twelve, has to encounter insuperable difficul-
ties.   But one of these will be quite enough.   Could an archbishop, who from the bottom of his heart believed that according to Holy Scripture and the Articles of his Church, the
apostleship of the Twelve is not transferable, yet actually
transfer that apostleship by ordination on a candidate who, on as
sure grounds and with as much confidence, held the same views
on the point in question as his ordainer ?   The one ordaining
repudiating the intention of conferring the Apostleship of the
Twelve, the one being ordained repudiating the intention of
receiving it.   Is the transfer of such an apostleship, supposing
there is any reality in it, under such circumstances safe and
sure ?   This is an interesting question for high Anglicans.

But before we quite leave Cyprian, it will be well to notice
how Dr Pusey has manipulated the language of Cyprian, and
thereby transformed him into a witness in favour of his own
doctrine.   In his preface to the epistles of Cyprian, after
claiming a multitude of things for this illustrious African
bishop which he never claimed for himself, he represents him
as "deriving his authority by vicarious *succession* from the
Apostles" (p. xiv.); intending his reader to understand, of

course, the twelve Apostles.   In proof of this we are referred to the passage in the writings of Cyprian which has already occupied our attention, viz., " Christ, who says to the apostles, and thereby to all prelates (rulers), who by vicarious *ordination* are successors of the apostles, ' He that heareth you,' &c. (Luke x. 16)." These, as we have seen, were the seventy apostles to whom, in the opinion of Cyprian, both bishops and presbyters were successors by a vicarious *ordination* (*vicaria ordinatione*), not *succession*; and the ordination, that is, appointment or making, in the judgment of Cyprian, as we have seen, was done by the free choice of his people.

In passing from Cyprian to later witnesses in the Church, the famous Council of Nice comes across our path, and demands *a.D.* a passing notice, especially as, in modern times as well as recently, in relation to an episcopal appointment, one of its canons has been employed, touching the very question of this paper.   Some have maintained, that according to this canon, bishops have the sole right of electing to the episcopal office. Others consider that the canon rather concerns the consecration than the election of bishops.   This diversity of opinion depends upon the interpretation of a word employed in the original, which, no doubt, in its ordinary use, and as expressly stated by Jerome and Chrysostom, means the ceremony of consecration—what, in fact, we now generally understand by the word ordination.   But it is notorious that there are exceptional cases, not only of the Greek word in this sense, but also in *ordinatio*, its Latin equivalent.   Illustrations of both have already come under our notice.   The Greek word is used by Eusebius in the comprehensive sense of constituting a bishop (see p. 27).   The Latin word *ordinatio*, as we have seen is used with the same extent of signification by Cyprian. Without quoting a number of authorities on this point, we shall only cite one, who is a host in himself.   Morinus, in his voluminous commentary on the ordinations of the Church, both ancient and comparatively modern, when explaining the general meaning of the word ordination (χειροτονία), as used by the Greeks, and the word ordination (*ordinatio*), as used by the Latins, expressly shows that the word in question, in rela-

tion to the Greeks, is sometimes used to denote election, and
in proof of this he refers to 2 Cor. viii. 19, where we find,
not the same word, but its corresponding verb, translated in
our version *chosen*.   For other proofs of this word being used
to signify election, he adduces the canon in question, as interpreted by Zonoras, and also the 19th canon of the Council of
Antioch and the 5th canon of the Council of Laodicea.   (Part
III., ch. ii. 5, p. 11.)

This much is certain, that whether or not we regard the canon
in question as requiring bishops to take part in the election or
consecration of a bishop, it in no wise sets aside or disannuls
the rights of the laity.   Our trustworthy authority Bingham
has spoken so well on this important point, that it shall be
our apology for giving his testimony.   He says,

" As to those who assert that the people were anciently indulged
in these matters before the Council of Nice, but that their power was
abridged by a new decree of that council, they are evidently under a
mistake; for it is certain the Nicene fathers made no alteration in
this affair, but left the whole matter as they found it.   For though
in one of their canons it is said that the presence, or at least the
consent of all the provincial bishops, and the confirmation or ratifi-
cation of the metropolitan shall be necessary to the election and
ordination of a bishop; yet that is not said to exclude any ancient
privilege that the people enjoyed, but only to establish the rights of
metropolitans and provincial bishops, which Meletius, the schismatical
Egyptian bishop, had particularly invaded, by presuming to ordain
bishops without the authority of his metropolitan, or consent of his
fellow bishops in the provinces of Egypt.   That nothing else was
designed by that canon, is evident from this, that the same council,
in the synodical epistle written to the Church of Alexandria, expressly mentions the choice of the people, and requires it as a condition of a canonical election.   For, speaking of such Meletian bishops
as would return to the unity of the Catholic Church, it says that
when any Catholic bishop died, Meletian bishops might succeed in
their room, provided they were worthy, and that the people chose
them, and the Bishop of Alexandria ratified and confirmed their
choice.   Our learned Bishop Pearson has rightly observed that
Athanasius himself was thus chosen after the Nicene Council was
ended, which is a certain argument that the people's right was not
abrogated in that council.   The Eusebian party made it an objection
against him, that he had not the choice of the people; but the bishops

of Egypt assembled in synod, in their synodical epistle do with great earnestness maintain the contrary, asserting that the whole multitude of the people of the Catholic Church, as if they had been all united in one soul and body, cried out, requiring Athanasius to be ordained bishop. When Gregory Nazianzen also says of him that he was brought to the throne of St Mark by the suffrage of all the people." (Book IV., ch. ii., sec. 11.)

At the second Council of Nice, 460 years after, the state of things had become entirely changed, for we are told by the learned Bishop Stillingfleet that "the second Council of Nice restrained the election only to bishops, which was confirmed by following councils in the Greek Church." (*The Unreasonableness of Separation*, p. 323.)

Dupin, in his History of the Church, referring to the same thing, says, "The third canon declares all the elections of bishops or priests, made by princes, to be void. It ordains that bishops shall be chosen by other bishops, and thereupon cites the canon of the Nicene Council, which does not speak of the election, but of the ordination of bishops. For of old time the election did belong to the clergy and people, and the ordination to the bishops." (Vol. i., p. 38.)

This second Council of Nice, held in the eighth century, shows how completely the people had at that time been deprived of their ancient rights, and to this day in the Greek Church they are still deprived of them. Bishop Wordsworth said, "I put this question to the Archbishop of Syra, 'What is the present condition of episcopal appointments in Greece?' and I found the condition to be this—that the bishops alone have a voice in the election." (*Speech in Convocation.*) May it never be so in the English Church.

Out of a multitude of instances in which the Christian laity was the chief agency in making bishops, three instances will be selected from the Latin Church. Augustine himself is the first instance. His promotion to be coadjutor and successor to his own bishop is recorded by Possidius as follows:—
"Megalius, Bishop of Calama, and primate for the time of Numidia, having come to Hippo upon a visitation, Valerius declared to the bishops then present, and *to all the people*, his

intention, which hitherto he had kept secret [viz., to have Augustine as his coadjutor and successor]; which when they had heard, with shouts and acclamations ardently desired it might be done." (*De Vita, cap.* viii.)

The second instance is recorded by Augustine himself, and as it is a fair specimen of an ancient election of a bishop, the account will be given rather fully:—

" When Bishop Augustine was sitting together with his fellow-bishops, Religianus and Martinianus, in the church of peace, in the region of Hippo, the presbyters, Saturninus, Leporius, Barnabas, Fortunatianus, Rusticus, Lazarus, and Eradius being present, and the clergy and the people in great numbers standing by . . . . Bishop Augustine said : I was lately in the church of Milevum, whither the brethren and servants of God who are there had requested me to come, because it was dreaded some tumult of the people might ensue after the death of my brother and fellow-bishop, Severus, of blessed memory. I went ; and the Lord of His great mercy granted that they did publicly receive him for their bishop, whom Severus had designed when alive ; for as soon as they came to understand the matter, they readily embraced the will of their dying bishop. Howbeit, some displeasure was taken, because somewhat too little was done by our brother Severus ; for he thought it might suffice that he should name his successor to the clergy : and hence he spoke nothing of it to the people, and so some of them were a little displeased. What need I insist more ? God was well pleased, the displeasure vanished, joy succeeded, and he whom the former bishop had named was ordained bishop. Therefore, that no person may complain of me, I here notify to you my intention or will, which I also believe is the will of God, and that is, I will that presbyter Eradius be my successor. It was acclaimed by the people, ' Thanks to God !' ' Praise to Christ !' was said twenty-three times. ' Hear, O Christ ! let Augustine live,' was said sixteen times. . . . . You see that both what I say, and what you say, is taken down in writing by the notaries of the Church ; neither my words nor your acclamations fall to the ground. That I may speak yet more plainly, we are just now framing an ecclesiastical deed; for I would willingly have this affair confirmed as strongly as it can be by men. It was acclaimed by the people thirty-six times. . . . . When silence was restored, Bishop Augustine said : I desire, as I said, to have my will and your will confirmed by an ecclesiastical deed, so far as it appertains to men ; and as to what belongs to the latent will of Almighty God, let us all pray that He may be pleased to confirm what

He hath wrought in us. It was acclaimed by the people. ' We give thanks for thy judgment,' was said sixteen times. ' Let it be done,' ' Let it be done,' was said twelve times. ' Thou art our father,' ' Eradius shall be bishop,' was said six times. When silence was restored, Bishop Augustine said : . . . . While my father and Bishop, the old man Valerius, of blessed memory, was yet in the body, I was ordained bishop, and sat with him ; but I knew not, neither did he know, that such a thing was prohibited by the council of Nice. What, therefore, was to be reprehended in me, I desire not to be reprehended in my son. . . . . He shall continue presbyter as he is, and he shall become bishop when it shall please God . . . . The instrument is now drawn up and finished, and you have given your consent and acclamations. Your approbation and acclamation are rehearsed . . . . I ask, in the last place, from you that as many of you as can will be pleased to subscribe this transaction ; here I shall need to have an answer from you ; let me have your answer, give me some acclamation in token of your assent. It was acclaimed by the people. ' Let it be done,' ' Let it be done,' was said twenty-five times. ' He is worthy,' ' He is just,' was said twenty-eight times. . . . . ' Hear, O Christ; preserve Eradius,' was said eighteen times."—(*Acta in Designando Aug. Successore Erad. epist.* CX., *tom.* ii., *pp.* 195, 196.)

Here we learn undoubtedly that in the time of Augustine the laity had the right of fixing who should, and who should not, be their bishop. This is admitted by Augustine, notwithstanding his knowledge of the council of Nice, and his willingness to follow its injunctions. He and his aged bishop, with whom he was coadjutor, had unknowingly violated one of its canons, by having two bishops constituted in one diocese or parish, whereas the canon says, "There may not be two bishops." The mistake that Severus, a neighbour bishop of Augustine, had made, in not recognizing the just rights of the laity, was one that Augustine would not repeat, and the means he took to avoid it are thus recorded. How far they were canonical, no canonists as yet have pronounced thereupon.

The last instance to be given is the popular election of Augustine's spiritual father, the illustrious Ambrose. Three or four early Church historians have recorded the event. The following is from Bishop Theodoret, the greatest and most valuable commentator of the century in which he lived :—

" Auxentius, Bishop of Milan, who had been excommunicated by
several councils on account of having embraced the errors of Arianism,
died . . . . The citizens assembled tumultuously, and contended
about the election. Those who had received the pernicious opinions
of Auxentius demanded to have a bishop of the same sentiments ;
while those who had adhered to sound doctrines desired a pastor of
the same faith as themselves. Ambrose, who was then governor of
the province, hearing of the dissensions, and fearing that a sedition
would ensue, hastened to the church. At his appearance, all dis-
putes ceased ; and the contending parties declared with one voice
that they chose Ambrose as their bishop. He had not then been
baptized. The emperor, on being informed of the election of the
people, ordered that the object of their choice should be immediately
baptized, and ordained ; for he was acquainted with the rectitude and
purity of his sentiments, and he regarded the unanimous consent of
the opposite faction as a proof of the Divine will.—(*Hist. Eccles., lib.*
iv., cap. v., vi. Opera, tom. iii., pp. 954, 955.)

Here, beyond all dispute, the people made Ambrose bishop.
But let us hear his testimony on the point. In discoursing
on Luke xviii. 20, relating to the law, he remarks, " This
introduction of the law is beautifully read for me to-day,
seeing it is the natal day of my priesthood. For every year
I seem to begin my priesthood anew, since it is renewed by
the age of time. This also is good which is read, ' Honour
thy father and mother.' For ye are my fathers, ye who conferred my priesthood ; ye, I say, are both sons and fathers:
sons individually, fathers collectively."—(*Comment. in Luc.,*
lib. viii., *tom.* iii., *col.* 186, 187.)

Such, then, is a portion of the arguments and evidence from
the earliest history of the making of bishops. It should be borne
in mind that Augustine, by the better portion of the Latin
Church, and by the whole body of our Protestant reformers,
has been almost regarded as if he were the middle and both
ends of all human Church authority. But supposing Augustine himself, his fathers, brethren, and disciples are all wrong,
that does not affect the value of their testimony for the purpose for which we require it. If they maintain that bishops
were chiefly created by those over whom they had to preside,
as they most certainly do, then with them the modern Anglican

opinion that bishops make bishops, by conferring in ordination the apostleship of the Twelve, could have formed no part of their belief. Many of our brethren who have no sympathy with high Anglican notions of making a bishop, yet nevertheless regard the office as of Christ's institution, and consider the human appointment to the sacred existing office rather to be made by bishops in ordination, than by the people in their election. With such, at present, we have no controversy ; our main object in this paper is to show that the transfer of the apostleship of the Twelve by ordination was unknown to the early fathers, and all that we have hitherto adduced from them has been in proof of this point.

We are now prepared to enter upon the second part of our subject, and undertake to show that the evidence adduced by high Anglicans to prove that the apostleship of the Twelve has been transferred by ordination to the present canonically ordained bishops, is worthless, if not contemptible. None of these high Anglicans maintain that the doctrine is revealed in Scripture ; they rather consider that it may be deduced therefrom, but they distinctly hold that it is plainly taught by the early fathers. These men, in common with Roman Catholics, profess to adopt a particular canon for the interpretation of Scripture, which we shall do well to notice. As stated by Bishop Wordsworth, it is as follows :—

"If there is such a thing as the church universal, to which Christ has promised His'presence and his Spirit ; if there are such words as the following in the New Testament, ' Lo, I am with you alway, even unto the end of. the world,' ' The comforter shall teach you all things, and guide you into all the truth,' &c. ; so, again, it is an illusory hope, that advances can be made in the work of sacred interpretation, by the instrumentality of any who reject the expositions of Scripture received by the consent of ancient Christendom, and who propound new interpretations invented by themselves, at variance with the general teaching of Scripture as received by the Catholic Church."—(*Preface to the Greek Testament, p.* ix.)

It remains now to give specimens of the manner in which they infer the doctrine of the transfer of the apostleship of the Twelve from Scripture. It shall be given as stated by two

authors, the Hon. W. E. Gladstone and Bishop Wordsworth. In addition to what we have already quoted from the former at page 4, he goes on to state :—

"After His ascension (?), 'Then said Jesus to them again, Peace be unto you ; as my Father hath sent me, even so send I you ; and when he had said this, he breathed on them, and saith unto them, Receive ye the Holy Ghost: whosesoever sins ye remit, they are remitted unto them; and whosesoever sins ye retain, they are retained.' (John xx. 21, 23.) But it naturally occurs that there is here no proof of the perpetuity of the apostolical power. It might have been needful, that for the first institution of the Christian Church a body of men should be appointed, with extraordinary qualifications, and with corresponding powers ; and yet it might have been ordained that their offices should determine with their lives, and that all subsequent exigencies of the body, which was to receive from them its first organization, should be provided for by such a machinery of government as its members might, in the due use of their understandings, conclude to be appropriate and sufficient for the purpose. But every such theory is at once and absolutely precluded by the closing words of St Matthew's Gospel, which are these : 'And lo ! I am with you alway, even unto the end of the world.' 'With *you* alway ;' but how should He be alway unto the end of the world with men whose lives were appointed to determine in the usual course of nature . . . . As our Lord had first instituted the office in the persons, so He now contemplates the office through the persons of the apostles ; and in declaring that He will ever abide with it, He declares and thereby establishes its perpetuity . . . . The power, therefore, by which the apostles acted was not to expire with their lives. It was to continue even to the end of the Christian dispensation."—(*Ibid.*, pp. 203-205.)

The latter, in addition to what we have already cited at page 16, states, " *With you*, and with those in whom your apostolic authority to preach and administer the sacraments will be continued to the end, and in whom, therefore, it will live by my power."—(*On Matt.* xxviii. 20.)

It should be well noted, how these two authors interpret and apply John xx. 21-23, so as to teach not only the Divine commission of the Twelve, but of the like commission to others who should come after them ; and, if possible, to confirm this erroneous opinion, they lay enormous stress upon Matt. xxviii.

20, which at first sight might seem to be in their favour. Others of the same school, in reference to this latter text, ask, with an air of triumph, " How could Christ be with them— that is, His apostles, alway—even to the end of the world, save and except in the persons of their successors ? "

Now, will it be believed that high Anglicans generally, as well as Bishop Wordsworth in particular, in so interpreting and applying the above texts, perpetrate the grossest possible violation of their own adopted canon. It may seem incredible, but it is nevertheless a fact. They do not even pretend to justify their misinterpretation by a single citation from any ancient witness, and for the best of all reasons, that out of the hundred huge folio tomes of patristic testimony, as yet not a single scrap has been discovered to justify any such interpretation and application. These ancient witnesses regard both texts as being addressed to others beside the Twelve, but especially Matt. xxviii. 20. This they consider to have been addressed to a multitude of disciples, as is shown in " Whose are the Fathers ? " How differently to modern high Anglicans the great Augustine and his disciple Tostatus applied John xx., 21-23, may be seen at pages 6, 9, 14 of this paper. As many extracts as would make a volume might be cited from the fathers, in which with one accord they apply Matt. xxviii. 20 to all believers. Thus, beginning with Origen in the third century, we find him saying, " Who saith to all in every place, ' Lo, I am with you always, even unto the end of the world ;' " and ending with Paschasius in the ninth century, whom we find representing the text as imparting " great confidence to all who believe in Christ, for He did not promise this only to His disciples, but also to all Christians ;" connecting those two with such links as Cyprian, Novatian, Athanasius, Hilary the bishop, Macarius, Jerome, Ruffinus, Augustine, Gaudentius, Chrysostom, Cyril of Alexandria, Leo I., Theodoret, Fulgentius, and Bede, all of whom give one and the same interpretation, and the chain of evidence is perfect and complete. The unanimous consent of all antiquity is exactly contrary to the assumptions of high Anglicans of the present day in regard to those texts teaching the transmission of the apostleship of the Twelve to the end of the gospel dispensation.

Before leaving this point, we must bring their own canon to bear upon it. Set off as it is in fine bold type, commandingly displayed in the preface, the most important part of a book, it seems adapted to perform admirable execution, but unfortunately it is most ruinous to its owners. Only conceive what, in their belief, depends upon the veritable transmission of the apostleship of the Twelve to our present bishops. But for this, we, like "the Presbyterian community of Scotland," as Dean Hook calls it, should have no Church, no valid ministry, no sacraments, and therefore no divinely authorised means of salvation. The succession of the apostleship of the Twelve. is with our high Anglican brethren a matter of infinite moment, and they make it depend, as we have seen (pp. 16, 44), upon two texts, and, according to their own canon, these two texts as interpreted by the Catholic Church. The consequences of an illusion, or "an illusory hope," on a point of such moment, must be tremendous in the extreme. Now, we find Bishop Wordsworth, and many brethren of his school, too numerous to mention in this short paper, "rejecting the expositions [of two important texts] of Scripture received by the consent of ancient Christendom, and propounding new interpretations, [partly] invented by themselves [and partly by others, probably since the Reformation], at variance with the general teaching of Scripture as received by the Catholic Church." Now, Bishop Wordsworth, in the very emphatic manner we have described, declares that so to interpret Scripture "is an illusory hope," yet he actually indulges in this illusion in a matter to him which, according to his creed, is of infinite moment. Is it said that this canon, though common to our high Anglican brethren, is private as regards the Catholic Church, having never been surveyed by it? Here, then, follows one which has been surveyed, is approved, is famous among our high Anglican brethren, and often employed by them when they consider it may be done with safety. "*Quod ubique, quod semper, quod omnibus creditum est.*" We emphatically maintain that the interpretatiom of Matt. xxviii. 20, in rela-

tion to all believers, and not exclusively to any class of ministers in the Church, is what has been believed everywhere,
always, and by all." That the interpretation put upon the
same text, so as to apply it exclusively to a particular class of
ministers, through whom the apostleship of the Twelve has
been handed down, is what has not been believed everywhere,
always, and by all. To speak still more plainly, it is what
has nowhere, never, and by nobody been believed, until comparatively modern times.

Now, this is a most serious charge against our high Anglican brethren; but we must not suppose, that because in this
case they do not cite a single father in defence of their interpretation, that they never cite them. The present instance is
a peculiar one. It is believed that they had not a scrap even
of seeming evidence to cite. But Bishop Wordsworth, and
such writers as the Hon. and Rev. A. P. Perceval, and the
Rev. H. J. Rose, pretend to cite evidence from some of the
fathers in proof of the apostleship of the Twelve being transferred to others. But they are justly chargeable with treating
patristic testimony unfairly. This is very fully and clearly
shown in the book "Whose are the Fathers?"

We shall only notice the testimony of one more witness in
favour of high Anglicanism. The present Bishop of Winchester, in one of his generally excellent "addresses to the
candidates for ordination," the last, entitled "Obedience to
Ordinary, &c.," remarks—

" (1.) Those of you who have read with any care the writings of
St Ignatius, must remember how frequently repeated are his exhor-
tations on this head [*Obedience to Ordinary*], as, for instance, to the
Church at Smyrna, ' Let all follow the bishop as the Apostles.' (2.)
And again, in his letter to Polycarp, ' Give heed unto the bishop,
that God may give heed to you.' (3.) And to the same effect speak
the succeeding fathers, amongst whom, as bearing remarkably on the
special point with which we are now concerned, I may remind you
of Tertullian's words, ' Dandi quidem (baptismum) habet jus, sum-
mus sacerdos, qui est episcopus: de hinc presbyteri, et diaconi; *non
tamen sine episcopi auctoritate;*' in which words he expresses the
then universally admitted principle that the priesthood and diaconate
derived their authority from the apostolical commission, given to the

episcopate, (4.) which accordingly he traces up to St John himself, where, speaking of the succession of bishops, he says, ' Habemus et Joannis alumnas ecclesias. . . . . Ordo . . . . episcoporum ad ori- ginem recensus in Joannem stabit auctorem.' . . . . (5) The same principle pervades others of the earliest writers; as, for instance, where St Jerome, that stout maintainer of the rights of presbyters, expressly declares, ' Thence it has come to pass, that without the command of the bishop neither the presbyter nor deacon has the right of baptising.' (6.) And St Ambrose adds, ' Though the pres- byters may have done this, yet is the beginning of their ministry from the highest priest—a *summo sacerdote,* an expression explained, as we have seen, by Tertullian to mean the bishop." (Pp. 241, 242.)

What the bishop has adduced from antiquity in proof of bishops having the apostolic commission of the Twelve, occu- pies a little more than the space of a duodecimo page. It is short, then, very much to the point—nothing could be more so. He begins well, improves as he proceeds, and ends triumphantly. Of course the bishop, as a wise and practical man, would give in this terse and telling form what in his opinion would be the best portion of the proofs commonly adduced by high Anglicans in favour of the transmission of the apostleship of the Twelve. Here, then, we have in these few sentences the result of the bishop's learning, general shrewdness, and best judgment, as to the most valuable part of the evidence on which, as we have seen, high Anglicans build so very much. But now come the questions—Are the statements of this piece of episcopal eloquence as much cha- racterised by correctness as confidence ? Are they as faithful as fluent ? Do they contain facts or fictions ? We shall now proceed to examine them. For convenience sake we shall divide them into two classes—statements original, and state- ments not so. Those of the first kind will be found under secs. 1, 2, and 6, as given above ; and they contain five pure fictions. (1) Ignatius does not say, "Let all follow the *bishop,*" but " Let all follow the *presbytery,*" as the apostles. (2) Ig- natius has no reference whatever to either deacons or presby- ters following any one. (3) He does not call upon either deacons or presbyters to give heed to the bishop. (4) In the passage to which we are referred, Ambrose makes no mention of baptism, but of the washing of feet ; (5) and by the highest priest he means the Lord Jesus Christ Himself. The epistle of Ignatius to the Smyrnæans to which we are referred was, as the preface, conclusion, and general contents show, addressed exclusively to the laity, and what he actually says is as follows : "See that ye all follow the bishop, even as Jesus Christ does the Father, and the presbytery as ye would the apostles ; and reverence the deacons, as being the institution of God." (Ch. viii.) The other passage to which we are referred is, "Give ye heed to the bishop, that God also may give heed to you. My soul be for theirs that are submissive to the bishop, to the presbyters, and to the deacons." (*To Polycarp*, ch. vi.) Not a syllable is here said of either presbyters or deacons giving heed to the bishop, but submission on the part of the laity is inculcated to bishop, presbyters, and deacons. What Ambrose states, with more of the context, is as follows :—

"Thou hast heard the lesson (John xiii. 4-15). The high priest was girded. [For although presbyters may also have done this, yet is the beginning of the ministry from the high priest.] The high priest, being girded, I say, has washed thy feet. What is this mystery [sacred sign]? Thou hast heard, then, that the Lord, when He had washed the other disciples' feet, came to Peter, and Peter said to Him, ' dost thou wash my feet ?'" (*De Sacramentis, lib.* iii., *cap.* i., *tom.* iv., *col.* 362.)

The statements not original are contained in secs. 3, 4, 5, as given above. In this garbled form they have often been made, and as often answered, since the time of Bishop Jewel.

We shall give both Tertullian and Jerome the opportunity of explaining their statements in their own words. Beginning with Tertullian, the part the bishop has cited from him, as given in sec. 3 above, will be placed in brackets and translated, and by this means a modern high Anglican bishop will be confronted with a sable African presbyter of very early antiquity, and the reader, it is thought, will see how great the difference of opinion was in the second century respecting the origin of episcopal power, compared with the opinion of high Anglicans in the nineteenth century.

D

" To conclude my little work, it remaineth that I give an admonition also concerning the right rule of giving and receiving baptism. [The right of giving it indeed hath the chief priest, which is the bishop; then the presbyters and deacons, *yet not without the authority of the bishop,*] for the honour of the Church, which being preserved, peace is preserved. Otherwise laymen have also the right, for that which is equally received may equally be given, unless the name disciples denote at once bishops or priests or deacons. The word of God ought not to be hidden from any; wherefore also baptism, which is equally derived from God, may be administered by all. But how much more incumbent on laymen is the duty of reverence and modesty! Seeing that these things belong to those of higher estate, let them not take upon themselves the office of the bishoprick set apart for the bishops. Emulation is the mother of divisions. A most holy apostle hath said, 'all things are lawful, but all things are not expedient.'" (*De Baptismo, cap.* xvii., *Opera*, p. 225.)

But to do the bishop justice, we ought, in all fairness, to give his gloss on the passage he cited, as given above in brackets, with his italics. He says, " In which words Tertullian expresses the then universally admitted principle that the priesthood and diaconate derived their authority from the apostolical commission, given to the episcopate." Could anything, by any possibility, be more contradictory to the plain teaching of Tertullian? So far from representing the bishop as having received any apostolical commission, he represents him as being allowed to have the power of baptizing for the honour of the Church, but maintains that every layman has the right to baptize, and that the rights conceded to the bishop have been conceded for the peace of the Church, on the ground of expediency. Bishop Kaye affirms, " In this passage the inherent right of the laity to baptize is expressly asserted." Then Bishop Wilberforce, as if his own gloss had transformed Tertullian's statement into an exactly opposite meaning, says, " which apostolical commission he traces up to St John himself, where, speaking of the succession of bishops," &c.

We are now brought to the fourth section of our extract from the Bishop; and his citation from Tertullian will be treated as the previous one :—

" On the whole, then, if that is evidently more true which is earlier; if that is earlier which is from the beginning; if that is from the beginning which has the apostles for its authors ; then it will certainly be quite as evident, that that comes down from the apostles, which has been kept as a sacred deposit in the churches of the apostles. Let us see what milk the Corinthians drank from Paul; to what rule (of faith) the Galatians were brought for correction ; what the Philippians, the Thessalonians, the Ephesians read out of it : what utterance also the Romans give, so very near, to whom Peter and Paul conjointly bequeathed the gospel, even sealed with their own blood. [We have also John's foster churches.] For although Marcion rejects his apocalypse, [the order of bishops, when traced up to their origin, will yet rest in John as their author.]—(*Adversus Marcionem, lib.* iv., *cap.* v., *p.* 406.)

Tertullian makes no reference whatever to a commission being handed on from the apostles through bishops. He is speaking of the handing down of Divine truth. Succession, as described by himself, was in no respect essential to a church being considered apostolic ; for he teaches that a church is not the less apostolical without it, provided it has the *doctrine* of the apostles. Thus he says :—

"Although churches can bring forward as their author no one of the apostles, or of apostolic men, as being of much later date, and indeed being founded daily ; nevertheless, since they agree in the same faith, are, by reason of their consanguinity in doctrine, counted not the less apostolical."—(*De Præscrip. Hæret, cap.* xxxii., *p.* 210.)

Bishop Kaye states: "By the expression *Ordo Episcoporum,* he did not mean *Order of Bishops,* as distinct from priests and deacons ; but the succession of bishops in the churches founded by St John," (p. 234.)

We now come to the fifth section of our extract from the Bishop. Here we shall treat the testimony of the learned Jerome after the same manner as we have done that of Tertullian, giving the Bishop's choice quotation in brackets:—

"But if you object, why does one who is baptized in the Church, by the imposition of the hand of the bishop only, receive the Holy Ghost, which we assert is given in true baptism ? Learn that this observance is derived from that authority, viz., that the Holy Ghost descended after the ascent of our Lord. Yet, in many places, this was done rather for the honour of the chief priesthood, than for an absolute necessity of the thing. Otherwise, if the Holy Ghost is poured down only by means of the prayer of the bishop, those men are in a deplorable condition, who were baptized in villages and castles, or other remote places, by presbyters and deacons, and who died before the bishop came to visit them. The safety of the Church depends on the dignity of the highest priest, on whom, if a certain supereminent power be not conferred, there will be in the churches as many schisms as priests. [Thence it has come to pass that without] the Chrism and [the command of the bishop neither the presbyter nor the deacon has the right of baptizing]. But we know that it is even lawful for a layman to baptize, if necessity required. For as one receives, so also can he give."—(*Adver. Lucifer, tom.* ii., *p.* 139.)

Here, beyond all question, Jerome teaches the very same doctrine as Tertullian. Bishop Jewel, 300 years ago, in answer to the papist Harding, who had quoted this very passage after the manner of Bishop Wilberforce, remarked :—

" This place of St Jerome is notably well noted. But if it might have pleased M. Harding to note but the two lines that went before, he should soon have seen that this note was not worth the noting. . . . . Jerome treateth there of the order of confirmation, which he saith, by the usage of the Church, for quietness and unity was ministered only by the bishop, and not by any other priest ; and that he saith, ' More for the honour of the state of bishops, than for the necessity of the law.' "

Dr Pusey remarks on the two passages from Tertullian and Jerome, as follows :—

" The maxims of Tertullian are often so fascinating, from their very condensation, as readily to gain admission, although involving unperceived consequences. Thus even St Jerome admits the maxim that what a man hath received, that he may impart, which, although it may in cases of necessity apply to the immediate subject, holy baptism, would equally justify Presbyterian ordination."—(*Preface to the Writings of Tertullian, pp.* xv., xvi.)

Thus far we have fairly investigated " The laws of the universal Church," in regard to the making of bishops, as the question before Convocation requires ; but the same question includes " the laws of the Church of England," in regard to the same thing. We therefore now proceed to examine this part of the question, and as in the former instance, we more especially examined the period of history alluded to by Bishop Wordsworth, and made due inquiry respecting the supposed existence of a fact which he took for granted, viz., the transmission of the apostleship of the Twelve, so in this instance we shall pursue exactly the same plan.

The Bishop in Convocation stated, "I have been told, upon the authority of the late bishop of Exeter, who heard it from Lord Denman, that if a volume to which I am about to refer had been brought before the Court in the Hampden case, the Court would have been very much swayed by it." The passage of the book in question is, "The second point, wherein consisteth the jurisdiction committed unto priests and bishops by the authority of God's law, is to approve and admit such persons as (being nominated, elected, and presented unto them, to exercise the office and room of preaching the Gospel, and of ministering the sacraments, and to have the cure of jurisdiction over these certain people within this parish, or within this diocese), shall be thought unto them meet and worthy to exercise the same ; and to reject and repel from the said room such as they shall judge to be unmeet therefor, and unto the priests or bishops belongeth, by the authority of the Gospel, to approve and confirm the person which shall be, by the King's Highness or the other patrons, so nominated, elected, and presented unto them to have the cure of these certain people, within this said parish or diocese, or else to reject him, as was said before, for his demerits or unworthiness."

Now, whether this passage does or does not serve the purpose for which the Bishop cited it in Convocation, it is of immense service in our present inquiry, especially as it states the views of our Church authorities after they had cast off the Pope. The very wording of the portion cited, shows that in the minds of its authors, there was no essential difference between a priest and a bishop, and hence they speak of both as being but one office. Thus they say, "the jurisdiction committed unto priests and bishops by the authority of God's law (not by receiving the apostleship of the Twelve), &c., within this parish, or within this diocese," "and unto the priests or bishops belongeth, by the authority of the Gospel,

&c." If it is said that this is only probable we will now proceed to absolute certainty.

The same archbishops and bishops who approved of the sentiments cited by Bishop Wordsworth, in the above extract, at the same time, if not in the same book, under the heading "*A Declaration of the Functions and Divine Institution of Bishops and Priests,*" after having enumerated " certain inferior orders or degrees," it is stated, " Yet the truth is, that in the New Testament there is no mention made of any degrees or distinctions in orders, but only of deacons or ministers, and of priests or bishops ; nor is there any word spoken of any other ceremony used in the conferring of this sacrament, but only of prayer, and the imposition of the bishop's hands." (*Burnet.*)

Two or three years after this, in the year 1540, *Questions and Answers concerning the Sacraments, and the appointment and Power of Bishops and Priests,*" are drawn up by Archbishop Cranmer, three of which questions concern our present subject. In the ninth question, relating to the making of bishops, we are told, " The ministers of God's Word under his majesty, be the bishops, &c., as for example, the bishop of Canterbury, the bishop Duresme, the bishop of Winchester, the parson of Winwick, &c. . . . . In the admission of many of these officers, be divers comely ceremonies and solemnities used, which be not of necessity, but only for good order and seemly fashion ; for if such offices and ministrations were committed without such solemnity, they were nevertheless truly committed. And there is no more promise of God, that grace is given in the committing of the ecclesiastical office, than it is in the committing of the civil office."

" 10. Whether bishops or priests were first ? and if the priests were first, then the priest made the bishop ?

" The bishops and priests were at one time, and were not two things, but both one office in the beginning of Christ's religion.

" 11. Whether a bishop hath authority to make a priest by the Scripture, or no ? and whether any other, but only a bishop, may make a priest ?

" A bishop may make a priest by the Scripture, and so may
princes and governors also, and that by the authority of God
committed to them, and the people also by their election ; for
as we read that bishops have done it, so Christian emperors
and princes usually have done it ; and the people, before
Christian princes were, commonly did elect their bishops and
priests.

" 12. Whether in the New Testament be required any consecration of a bishop and priest, or only appointing to the
office be sufficient ?

" In the New Testament, he that is appointed to be a bishop
or a priest, needeth no consecration by the Scripture ; for
election or appointing thereto is sufficient." (*Works of
Cranmer*, vol. II., pp. 116, 117.)

Nothing by any possibility could be more fatal to the high
Anglican conceit of the transmission of the apostleship of the
Twelve by bishops.   These men had cast aside the single
sham apostle of Rome, and modern shams pretending, and
others pretending for them, to have the exact apostleship of
the Twelve, explained as consisting of "the same apostolic,
episcopal, and pastoral office," as those exercised by Christ
Himself (see page 16), were not in the Church of England
until many years after this.

Is it urged that we are quoting sentiments from bishops of
the English Church while they were in a state of transition and
before the Reformation was effected.   We have no wish to
follow the practice of some of our high Anglican brethren in
quoting "Our Protestant fathers in the sixteenth century,"
before they were either Protestant or Reformed, and according
to Roman fashion, roasted men alive for denying the blasphem-
ous doctrine of Transubstantiation. (see *Whose are the Fathers?*
pp. 312, 313.)   But we distinctly maintain that these very
men who, as we have seen, made no real distinction between a
bishop and a presbyter, as of divine appointment, did, about the
time the Reformation was approaching completion, frame an
Ordinal in the year 1549, which remained in use until 1661,
in which any real distinction between a presbyter and a bishop
in ordination, is ignored. This Ordinal differs from any previous

one, and is peculiar to itself. The case of Timothy, both in the ordering of priests and the consecration of bishops, is the model adopted.   If Timothy was ordained twice, once as presbyter and again as bishop, then the Ordinal in question makes a real distinction between a presbyter and a bishop. But if St. Paul only ordained Timothy once as presbyter or bishop, and when he called him to still further work, and reminded him of the ordination he had already received, then this same ordinal makes no distinction between a bishop and presbyter.   The question, is when St. Paul said to Timothy "Stir up the gift of God which is in thee by the putting on of my hands," (2 Tim. i. 6,) did he promote him from the office of a presbyter to that of a bishop?   No one pretends that he did.   Dean Hook, in his "Church" (or rather, as it ought to be called, modern high Anglican or Tractarian Church) Dictionary," teaches under the article *Ordination*, that Timothy was not ordained bishop when those words were uttered, but was so ordained at the time to . which those words allude, viz., when he received the gift that · was in him, with the laying on of the hands of the presbytery, (1 Tim. iv. 14.)   In the first Ordinal of our Reformed Church this was taken as the model in the ordination of a presbyter, and when a presbyter was consecrated a bishop, he was not considered to receive any new ordination.   "Take the Holy Ghost, and remember that thou stir up the grace of God which is in thee, by imposition of hands; for God hath not given us the spirit of fear, but of power, and love, and of sobernesss;" obviously citing the address of St. Paul to Timothy when not ordaining him again, but reminding him of the ordination he had already received (2 Tim. i. 6, 7.) For much more on this point, see "Whose are the Fathers?" chap vi. pp. 300-337.

It remains that we now come to some practical conclusion. From what has so recently transpired respecting the appointment of Dr. Temple as Bishop of Exeter, there can be no doubt but that a large majority of both clergy and laity take a **pro-found** interest in the question before Convocation ; and so far from wishing to abate that interest, we wish it were ten-fold more than it is, and especially in regard to the laity.

But what is the aim and object of our high Anglican brethren in discussing the question of the making of bishops? Bishop Wordsworth, their most able and successful representative shall tell us : "Let us look at the language of the Romish controversialists, with regard to the bishops of the Church of England. They stigmatize them as mere Act of Parliament bishops ; creatures and vassals of the civil power. If we were to forfeit our connection with the ancient universal Church, and to surrender its principles, we should weaken ourselves, and destroy our own foundations, and give a triumph to our enemies," (*Speech in Convocation.*) The sole aim and object in this enquiry is to demonstrate to the satisfaction of certain systems of gross superstition, such as those of Rome, Greece, and Abyssinia, which, as a matter of convenience, are commonly called Churches, that in all essential points we are one with them, and especially so in having the apostleship of the Twelve, and he admits that even the Roman Church, which he believes to be the Babylon of the Apocalypse, has this "sacred deposit," and that from thence it was received into the Anglican Church. When the Bishop deprecates "the forfeiture of our connection with the ancient universal Church," he really means our connection with the above named modern systems of superstition. With several other high Anglicans, Bishop Wordsworth has been actively engaged in endeavouring to effect an open junction of our Church with the Greek Church. Thus we hear of "The Eastern Church Association," as in existence some time before the year 1864, and in some way or other, it appears to have begun with the present Bishop of Winchester. For in the *Clerical Journal* of October 27, 1864, we are told: "The Rev. Dr. Fraser gave an interesting account of the origin of the Association, observing that it began through a letter written by the English Chrysostom, the Bishop of Oxford—for the English Church had its Chrysostom at Oxford." But in relation to this point, we obtain the most choice piece of information from a foreign newspaper—the *Moscow Gazette*, that a meeting was held at the S. P. G. Offices, in Pall Mall, "on the subject of a union with the Eastern Churches," on November 15, 1865. Prince N. Orloff, who was present on the occasion, informs us in his letter in the above-named paper, that the Bishop of

Oxford (now Bishop of Winchester) presided "on the occasion, and we are informed that among other clergy, Dr. Pusey and Dr. Wordsworth were present, and that "the Bishop of Oxford urged that, deferring all dogmatical debates, we should proceed to celebrate the Lord's Supper by intercommunion, if such were the wish of the chiefs of our Church. Prince Orloff moved among other things, "That works should be published in England, setting forth the history, doctrine, and present condition of the Anglican Church, with a view to proving that it is not a Protestant, but a Catholic Church, and, accordingly, related to the Eastern church."

The progress towards unprotestantizing the English Church has of late been very considerable ; and the zeal of such men as the Bishop of Winchester and the Bishop of Lincoln to effect a junction with the Greek Church is too obvious at the present time to need any proof.

We cannot but notice, in passing, with what sweet assurance the Bishop of Winchester seemed to think that, if it were but the wish of the chiefs of the Church, as he calls them, without any further authority, they might effect an open union with the Greek Church. Not a word said about the wish of the priests ; and what is still more serious, not a word respecting the wish of the laity. He entirely overlooked, to use the language of Cyprian, "the dignity of the Catholic Church, and the faithful and uncorrupt majesty of the people within it." Cyprian was in principle a rabid Donatist, and arrogated to himself, as bishop, more than was his due ; and his disciples, who followed him in this respect, gave infinite trouble to the Church, as the writings of Augustine testify, and of which there are some striking proofs in this paper ; but yet, notwithstanding, Cyprian never did anything of importance without consulting the will of the people. The very idea of uniting in open communion the English Church, as she is at present constituted, with the Greek Church, and that without the free consent of the people, or that of their representatives, would, when viewed in the light of the teaching of the great Augustine, be as gross a dereliction of duty, as if certain persons, promoted by a modest and chaste woman, not to be her chiefs,

but chief servants, and bound to act according to the well-
known rules of her household ; but instead of so doing, were
to assume absolute authority, and actually proceed so far,
without even consulting the will of their mistress, as to associate
her with a "whorish baud of Babylon," or some Greek or
Abyssinian damsel of equally unquestionable character.

Of this we are morally certain, that if the question before
convocation is fully and fairly gone into, as far as the testimony
of the early Church. is concerned, the conclusion come to will
be that the people over whom the bishop had to preside were
chiefly his makers.

The connection of man and wife as instituted of God is not
an unsuitable illustration of the connection between a bishop
and his charge, as far as the making and completion of the
engagement is concerned. A church, in want of a bishop,
claimed and exercised the sole right of choosing one. Presbyters, or any other order of clergy, had no votes distinct from the
laity, but voted in common with them ; and the will of the
majority determined who was to be their bishop. The formal
union, however, was effected by neighbouring bishops, by the
ceremony of ordination. But if it should appear on good
grounds that the person chosen was defective in faith or
morals, the rite was withheld, and the people probably would
have to choose again. But perhaps it may be said that he who
performs the marriage ceremony makes the man a husband to
the wife, and that they who perform the holy rite of ordination
make a man the bishop of his church. This is all that can
be said in favour of bishops making bishops. But then it
should be understood in both instances that the man who is
made the husband to the wife, and the man a bishop to the
church, are thus made by the free choice or acceptance, as the
case may be, of the wife and of the church. It should be
especially noticed that the early churches were sometimes very
deficient in their respect to the office of the minister of their
choice, and greatly abused the power they had. This may be
seen from the epistle of Clement, a portion of which is given
at page 20 above. We learn the same thing from the epistles
connected with the name of Ignatius, and hence his frequent

and urgent inculcation of obedience on the part of the people
to their clergy.   In point of fact, the Ignatian epistles show
the weakness of the episcopal power and the strength of that
of the laity, and their abuse of it.   Here we cannot but
notice, in passing, how fatal the testimony of Ignatius is to
the assumptions of high Anglicans.   These men, as we have
seen, claim for their bishop, and him only, the apostleship of
the Twelve.   Ignatius, whether we take only the three epistles,
supposed to be genuine, or the seven, whether of the shorter
or longer recensions, assigns to the presbyter, and him only,
the place of the apostles.   The following is the style in which
he speaks : " The bishop presiding in the place of God, and
the presbyter in the place of the council of the apostles."
" Be subject to the presbytery, as to the apostles of Jesus
Christ."   " Let all reverence   . . . .   the presbyters as
the council of God, and college of apostles."   " All follow the
bishop, as Jesus Christ the Father, and the presbytery as the
apostles."   From this time onward, the bishops gained in
power, and by the middle of the fourth century, to a great
extent had become an independent power.   At this time their
status and worldly position had become so entirely changed,
that at different councils they made canons avowedly to promote their worldly honour.   Thus, at the council of Sardica,
in the year 347, the sixth canon is to this effect : " It shall
not be lawful to place a bishop in a village, or small city,
where a single presbyter will be sufficient ; for in such places
there is no need to set a bishop, lest the name and authority
of bishops be brought into contempt."   Again, at the council
of Laodicea, about the year 365, in its 57th canon, we read :
" Bishops must not be appointed in villages and country dis-
tricts, but visitors ; those who have been heretofore appointed
must do nothing without the consent of the bishop of the
city."

Soon after this, the power claimed and exercised by the
people and clergy in electing their bishops was entirely lost ;
and though in most instances a form of election was continued,
more especially by the city presbyters of the diocese, yet, in
truth, they had no real choice in the matter.

One of the darkest spots in the early history of the Church is the riotous, bloody, and murderous scenes at the popular election of bishops. It would seem as if in those early times the common people exercised their power by instinct rather than reason, which served as an excuse for aspiring bishops and civil potentates to deprive them of it, and exercise it for them. How much better it had been, if, instead of robbing them of their just rights, these now stronger parties had assisted the weaker in exercising their power by reason; as, for instance, through some few representatives periodically chosen by them. According to early antiquity, as we have seen, it was believed that the laity held these rights by divine authority.

The Reformers sought to restore these rights, as well as purge the Church from its corruptions. In bringing about these changes, they reverted to an earlier stage of its history, and employed some of the most eminent Christian authors of primitive times to pull down or to detach, as the case might be, any additions to the superstructure of the Church as were added by more recent authorities. By "our Reformers," is not meant those of the English Church merely, but those of all the Reformed Sister Churches, as our great and learned divines, piously and affectionately called them. Of these there were eleven, and our own Church made the twelfth. Each one of these Churches drew up a most elaborate and learned confession of faith. Bishop Jewel prepared the one representing the Church of England, and the whole thing was set on foot by Archbishop Cranmer.

These several confessions were duly published under the title of " The Harmony of Protestant Confessions, exhibiting the Faith of the Churches of Christ, Reformed after the pure and Holy Doctrine of the Gospel, throughout Europe."

Now, be it observed that the most illustrious Divines and Doctors of these Churches, as their writings now testify, appealed, not only to the Written Word, but to the early Church, in refutation of the superstitious errors of their opponents, and we are quite sure they did so successfully, and triumphantly, and we are morally certain that the peculiarities of high Anglicanism, if submitted to the same test, would share the same fate. We have no wish to shock the feelings of some of our modern evangelical brethren by the admission of such an appeal, and therefore, we shall say a few words in defence of it. Evangelicals of the present day, contrary to their learned and noble ancestors, the leading Reformers, have an unfounded prejudice against any appeal to the early fathers in matters of faith and practice, and are actuated by the supposition that they would obtain from them an unfavourable verdict. Consequently, the fathers are deprecated as witnesses, and a variety of charges is too commonly preferred against them, by way of putting them out of court. No class of men better represent the opinions of the party to which they belong than editors and reviewers ; and from these we may best learn in what estimation an appeal to the fathers is held by certain earnest and sincere Christian men. One editor declined to review the book, " Whose are the Fathers ? " alleging as a reason what follows, " At present our readers are very little concerned to know what were the opinions of the Fathers on the controversies, which aim at the vitals of the Church. We must go at once to the fountain head." A second, while speaking well of the book, nevertheless says, " But the author has taken very dangerous ground, and exposed himself and his cause to serious risk. Undoubtedly, it is easy to draw up a *catena patrum*, in which Anglican views are condemned, but it is equally easy to prepare another in an opposite sense, that shall appear to be equally decisive. We must confess our surprise that Evangelicals should ever be content to compromise their own position, by admitting an appeal to any authority, but that of Scripture." Mr Harrison would tell us, doubtless, that he has carefully guarded himself against the idea that the teachings of the fathers are to be accepted as decisive, and that while showing how weak is the case of Anglicans, even if their own canon of interpretation, as given by Dr Wordsworth, be admitted, he has distinctly protested against its adoption. Still, we cannot but feel that in a conflict of authorities, the Anglicans can make out a strong case in support of their own system. It is fair to say, however, that Mr Harrison has at all events shown that antiquity is not so unanimous in their favour as they would have the world to believe. His work is of a most learned and exhaustive character, and he has certainly astonished us by the great weight of evidence which he has accumulated in support of his own views." A third reviewer remarks, "Evangelical clergymen are on ticklish ground when they appeal to patristic writers. Anglicans have the best of it in that field. . . . . Like all such things, it (*the catena*) is rather one-sided."

This reviewer, judging from general custom, concludes that "the catena is rather one-sided;" and one of the others conceives that "it is equally easy to prepare another in an opposite sense, that shall appear equally decisive." In reply to this, it is stated : "In the first part of the catena will be found all, or nearly all, the passages usually quoted by these Anglo-Catholics and their sympathizers in favour of their view of the doctrine. We have not knowingly omitted one extract of that kind which has come under our notice" (p. 11). And now, after further reading and investigation, we question whether it can be said with truth that a single quotation of any importance has been omitted from any father, which has been used by Romanizers or Romanists in defence of their teaching in regard to the office of the Christian ministry.

High Anglican and Ritualistic reviewers, who have specially alluded to the catena, have made no charge against it as being one-sided. In the *Church and State Review*, edited by Archdeacon Denison, it is stated, "The *Catena Patrum* must have cost him a considerable amount of patient toil, as well as of time." The *Ecclesiastic* states, " It (the book) is well and carefully put together, the Catena applying clearly to and explaining the text. The selections from the Fathers are, on the whole, fairer than the second Catena." The *Church Review* writes, " The arrangement and method of the book are capital, and the application of the Catena to the text is excellently managed. We find long extracts from the Fathers of the Church, collected with considerable care and fairly translated." The *Guardian* says, "Mr. Harrison fairly puts down the passages which are dead against him; and so applies to some extent his own antidote."

From this we learn how exceedingly sensitive some of our evangelical brethren are as to making any appeal whatever to the Fathers, and how utterly they are wanting in confidence of any appeal their friends may make to them. Let it be distinctly understood that we do not accept their teaching as in any way binding on our own conscience, but the Scriptures alone. Not so high Anglicans, who regard the fathers as of equal authority with the Scriptures, or rather they only accept the Scriptures as interpreted by the early Church, meaning the early fathers. We cannot well argue with them on our principles, inasmuch as they do not admit them. But what objection can there be to argue with them on their own principles? We do not admit the authority to which they appeal as in any way binding on us; but we can easily distinguish between the authority ascribed to the fathers and what they have recorded as matters of fact and religious doctrine. The former, the high Anglican admits as binding upon himself, but we admit no such thing; the latter resolves itself into a matter of history: and now comes the question, Do the early fathers teach, or do they not, what high Anglicans ascribe to them on the office of the Christian ministry? We maintain emphatically that they do not, in proof of which we allege the book "Whose are the Fathers?" We maintain, moreover, that the same high Anglican doctrines are contrary to the standards and the great doctors of the English Church of the latter half of the sixteenth century, and that these also corroborate our use and application of the fathers as against such doctrines as those held on the Christian ministry, in proof of which we also allege the book "Whose are the Fathers?"

But to return to the immediate point in hand, viz., the question before convocation. We think evidence enough has already been adduced to show that, if bishops are rightly made —that is, according to Scripture precedent and early antiquity —the people over whom the bishop is to preside should be the principal parties in choosing him. With regard to the authority of Scripture on this point, Mason, in his book "*On the Consecration of the Bishops in the Church of England*," says, "Wo find three varieties of the election of ministers in the New Testament. The first by lots; the second by voices; the third by the spirit of prophecy. Matthias was chosen by lots ; the deacons by voices ; Timothy and others by the spirit of prophecy. For, as Chrysostom saith : " In those days, the pastors were made by prophecy : what is, by prophecy ? by the Holy Ghost : as Saul was shewed by prophecy, when he lay hid among the stuff, as the Holy Ghost said, ' Separate me Paul and Barnabas, so was Timothy chosen.' Theodoret : ' Thou hast not thy calling from men, but thou receivedst that order by divine revelation.' Oecumenius : ' By revelation of the Spirit, Timothy was chosen of Paul to be a disciple, and ordained a bishop.' This kind of election seemeth to be usual in the apostles' times, and to have continued so long as the gift of prophecy and discerning of spirits remained. Now of these three, the first and the third were by God himself ; the second by all the faithful. This is all we find in Scripture." (*Lib.* iv., ch. 4, p. 158.)

Then, as respects the testimony of the early Church, Clement expressly asserts that rulers were appointed " with the consent of the whole Church," (page 20.) . It is presumed that of the three, modes of election above named, that by the people only was continued. Cyprian, as we have seen, considered that it was by this act that the will of God was ascertained, (see pp. 29, 31, 32.) Remigius states the same thing, (page 33.) The election of Fabian was considered an especial token of the will of God, (page 27); and also that of Ambrose, (page 42.) Augustine, Jerome, and Ruffinus distinctly affirm that the Church constituted or created bishops, (pp. 15, 16, 18, 19.) That this constituting or creating was principally effected by their being elected by the people, we have given incontrovertible evidence, both before and after the Council of Nice. Dupin, a very competent, and, on this point, an impartial authority, in his "Abridgment of the Discipline," in relation to the history of the Church in the third century, says, "They took great care, in the choice of their ministers, to elect such persons whose life and conversation were unblameable. After the death of those who had been ordained by the apostles, the people elected." Again, in his "Abridgment of the Discipline of the fourth age of the Church," he says, "When a bishop died, all the bishops of the province were called together to ordain a successor in his room. He was commonly chosen by the clergy and people of the vacant church."

The reason why the laity should elect their bishops, rests on the fact that the seat of all power and authority is placed in the Church, as Firmilian states, (page 18,) Augustine proves, (pp. 8-10,) and Tostatus so elaborately illustrates, (pp. 5-7.) Hooker himself says, "The whole Church visible being the true original subject of all power," and teaches that the authority of bishops, which they have by the force of custom rather than by any true and heavenly law, is "a sword which the Church hath power to take from them," (*Book* vii. 5.)

We conclude with certainty that bishops, receiving from one another the apostleship of the Twelve, with all its peculiar powers and prerogatives, was no doctrine of the ancient Catholic Church, nor is it the doctrine of the Church of these realms.

We look forward with interest, then, to the consideration of the proposition now before Convocation: "That a joint-committee of both Houses of Convocation be appointed to examine and report upon the laws of the universal Church, and also the laws of the Church of England, concerning the election, confirmation, and consecration of Bishops; and that it be instructed to offer such remarks and recommendations thereupon as the said joint-committee may think best."

We are certain that if this proposition is fully and faithfully considered, the high Anglican conceits respecting bishops, "having been commissioned to execute the same apostolic, episcopal, and pastoral office" as Christ himself executed, and that this office has come down from Christ through an unbroken line of ordainers to the present English bishops, if considered at all, will be condemned by both Houses of Convocation.

This, then, having been settled to be no mark at all of a true Church, least of all a necessary mark, but rather, as held by Rome, is a mark of the beast, there will be no desire to have such a mark, nor to associate ourselves with others who pretend to have it. In fact, so far from wishing to form a union with these Roman, Greek, and Abyssinian Christians, their vain and unfounded pretensions, together with their confessedly gross corruptions of the Christian faith, must be an effectual bar thereto, and that we ought almost as soon to think of uniting ourselves with any remains that may be found in the dark places of the earth of the ancient Druidical system, as with these grievously erroneous systems of Christianity, so called, until they shall be reformed.

The committee has a very delicate and difficult task before it, especially so, if their report and recommendation are to meet the approbation of our high Anglican brethren. The hierarchical element, which during the last quarter of a century has become very much developed, has, in a late episcopal appointment, been brought into collision with the lay element in the Church of England, and has been worsted; and hence advice or redress is sought where perhaps it was most natural to seek it, viz., in Convocation.

The point to be decided, as far as high Anglicans are concerned, is this: Are bishops, as regarded from their point of view, independent rulers of the Church? Do they derive authority from the Church? or do they derive it by a vicarious succession from the apostles? Have bishops entrusted to them plenary powers over the Church, transmitted to them from the Twelve? Did Christ grant a commission of a regency in the hands of bishops to be a perpetual commission until His return? Substituting a plain phrase for this high Anglican nomenclature, Are bishops the masters of the Church? or is the Church their mistress, and they her chief servants? These are points on which the Committee of Convocation will have to report, and offer such remarks and recommendations thereupon as it may think best.

The most serious difficulty that stands in the way of our high Anglican brethren is the substantial, real fact of the Reformation, which has practically determined that the Church is the mistress, and that her officers perform their functions by her sanction and authority. The Reformation, wherever it took effect, was a death-blow to an absolute hierarchy, and so violent was the reaction from priestly domination to laical freedom, and even authority, that the order and name of those who had been the chief rulers of the Church, if not from the beginning, yet from a very early period, was entirely swept away. Our own Church was the only exception, and that arose principally from this cause, that instead of the Reformation proceeding from the middle class of society, as it usually did, it took its rise from the supreme powers and the nobility generally. After the laity were deprived of their power, it was exercised partly by the bishops, and partly by the civil authorities in those parts where they were called by the Christian name. In fact, as the history of our own country testifies, there was a constant strife between the civil and the ecclesiastical authorities in regard to fixing who should be bishop to any vacant see. Whatever the popes of Rome might pretend as to their being successors to all the powers of St. Peter, many of them—if apparently authentic history does not tell lies—proved themselves to be virtual successors to Simon Magus. The amount of money which the Roman popes extorted from this country is almost fabulous. The following are the two last items of papal exactions, as recorded by Mason in his book "*On the Consecration of the Bishops in the Church of England, &c*," "In the yeere 1532, inquisition was made of Papall expilations, and it was found that in the foure yeeres last past, *the Roman Court had received for investitures of Bishops*, 160,000 *pounds*. In the yeere 1533 the Pope had of Cranmer for his Bulles concerning his Consecration and his Pall, 900 duckets, and the same yeere his usurped authority was banished out of England" (*Lib*. iv., *ch*. 13.)

Be it observed that when the Pope was cast aside no priestly ecclesiastic was appointed to take his place, and so far was the Church of England from supposing that it was essential to the being of a Church to have one man, or an order of men, who were supposed to possess the same apostolic, episcopal, and pastoral office of that of the Twelve, in her nineteenth Article, where the marks of a Church are given, Church discipline or government of any kind, is not one of them. As this is a most important point, and that there may be no mistake respecting it, we shall give the testimony of one of the best authorized expositions of the Articles which our Church possesses, and as the title of the book itself is replete with the kind of information high Anglicans require, and is in accordance with the real aim and object of this paper, we shall give it in full: "The Faith, and Doctrine, and Religion, professed and protected in the Realm of England, and dominions of the same : expressed in 39 Articles, concordably agreed upon by the reverend Bishops and Clergy of this Kingdom, at two several meetings, Convocations of theirs, in the years of our Lord 1562 and 1604 : The said Articles analyzed into propositions, proved to be agreeable both to the written Word of God, and to the extant Confessions of all the neighbour Churches Christianly reformed. The adversaries also of note, and name, which from the Apostles' days, and primitive Church hitherto, have crossed or contradicted the said Articles in general, or any particle, or proposition arising from any of them in particular, hereby are discovered, laid open, and so confuted. Perused, and by the lawful authority of the Church of England allowed to be public. Rom. xvi. 17, 'I beseech you brethren, mark them diligently, which cause divisions and offences, contrary to the doctrine which ye have received and avoid them.' Printed by John Legatt, Printer to the University of Cambridge. 1607."

Rogers, the author of this exposition on the point for which we are citing him, in his fifth proposition of the 19th Article, says, "The marks and tokens of the visible Church are the due and true administration of the word and sacrament. The proof from God's Word. There is the visible Church of Christ, where the Word of God sincerely is preached, and the sacraments instituted by our Saviour are duly administered." After giving Scripture proofs, he states, "The Christians in all reformed Churches acknowledge these things." In establishment of this point, he cites from the "Harmony of Confessions," of which we have given some account at page 61, and then remarks, "Some (and they also many of them very godly men) add ecclesiastical discipline for a note of the visible Church.

But because the said discipline in part is included in the marks
here mentioned, both we, and in effect, all other well-ordered
Churches, over pass it in this place, as no token simply of the
visible Church . . . The errors and adversaries unto this
truth.   We renounce, therefore, as altogether unsound and
anti-christian, the opinions of the Papists, who both deny the
pure preaching of God's Word, and the administration of the
sacraments among Protestants, to be the marks of Christ, His
visible Church ; and affirm the tokens hereof to be antiquity,
unity, universality, succession, &c., as doth Stapleton, Bristow,
Bozius, Hill, and Alabaster [and for the most part all high
Anglicans.]

Under the sixth proposition he states, "Besides that churches
visible and glorious have erred, it appeareth evidently by the
superstition, heresies, yea, and atheism now reigning at Jerusalem, Alexandria, and Antioch.   This with us the Churches
in their confessions do acknowledge."

Now if the Committee look into the real history of the
early Church, as well as that of the Church of England, they
will not attempt to prove or feign to believe that their Church,
like certain apostate Churches, makes the being of a Church
of Christ, the validity of the sacraments, the calling of the
ministry, and the means of salvation, dependent upon an unfounded fiction, which we forbear more definitely to charac-
terize.

If the Committee examine, as we trust they will, the history
of the visible Church as given in the New Testament, they
will find, beyond all question, that the body of the laity was a
real power.   Among other undoubted proofs, they will not
fail to notice this one,—that when St Paul wrote to a Christian Church, he always addressed his letters to the whole body,
never to the ministers : he did not usually name them.   There
is one exception, however, but that only confirms the rule.   Thus,
when writing to the Church at Philippi, he says, "Paul and Timo-
theus, the servants of Jesus Christ, to all the saints in Christ Jesus
which are at Philippi, with the bishops and deacons."   If the
question before Convocation be fully and fairly gone into, there
can be no mistake respecting the real power of the laity in

the primitive Church, though, from very early times, the laity of the Church of England, as well as the laity of other ancient Churches, was deprived of it. It may perhaps be said, with some show of reason, that the Church of England became her own mistress at the Reformation, and that she still holds the chief power, inasmuch as her lay representative has the chief power and government of the Church. In answer to this, it may be well said that we are thankful for past favours, and the amount of liberty and good order which we have enjoyed ; but we think that the present representation is inadequate for our present exigencies, whatever it might be when the Church and the government were almost one and the same body, and the laity of those days far less capable of exercising any power with which they might be entrusted. Might not the Committee of Convocation recommend something of this kind, that, as the Church of primitive times had a real power which they could exercise in the choice of their chief ministers, so the Church of England should have the same power in some measure restored—not, however, in the shape of popular elections of bishops, which in many instances were a sad disgrace to the Christian name ; but let the priests have certain representatives periodically chosen, let the laity at least have a double number of such representatives, and let these be constituted a real elective body—let the state nominate, let the bishops, as of old, formally unite the bishop elect to those who have chosen him, by the rite of solemn prayer, and the laying on of hands, commonly called ordination, provided they see no cause or just impediment to such a union according to the defined laws of the Church.

If these are the days of liberty, when wrongs are to be righted, what time so fitting as the present for the laity of the English Church to stand up for their liberty, and claim their just rights as granted by a divine charter, exercised by the same authority in the early Church, and now restored to many reformed Churches with the happiest and most successful results ?

If the illustrious and most learned Jerome could say, as we believe wisely and truly, in relation to the times in which he lived, and the state of the episcopate, which even then was twenty-fold more numerously represented than now, " The safety of the Church depends on the dignity of the highest priest, on whom, if a certain super-eminent power be not conferred, there will be in the Churches as many schisms as priests :" had he lived a few centuries later, he might have affirmed, with equal if not with more wisdom and truth, " The safety of the Church depends upon the body of the people, who, if they relinquish the keys of authority and power, which they inherently and by divine right hold, ' as the most noted bishop of the whole world, the truly holy and most blessed Pope Augustine' (ut episcopus in toto orbe notissimus . . . . vere sanctus et beatissimo papa Augustinus.—*Epist.* xi., *ad Augustinum*) teaches, the servants of the Church will become her masters, and the Church, their mistress, will become their slave, and as respects the laity, there will be for them as many houses of spiritual bondage as there are ████████."

TURNBULL AND SPEARS PRINTERS EDINBURGH.

TO BE PUBLISHED SHORTLY, BY SUBSCRIPTION,

.. *An octavo Volume of about* 700 *pages,*

ENTITLED

"AN ANSWER TO DR. PUSEY'S CHALLENGE RESPECTING THE DOCTRINE OF THE REAL PRESENCE,"

in which the Doctrines of the Lord's Supper, as held by him, Roman Catholics, Ritualists, and High Anglo-Catholics, are examined and shown to be contrary to the Holy Scriptures and to the Teaching of the Fathers of the First Eight Centuries, with the testimony of an ample *Catena Patrum* of the same period." By JOHN HARRISON, Vicar of Fenwick, near Doncaster, Author of " WHOSE ARE THE FATHERS ?" &c.

Price to Subscribers, Twelve Shillings.

Also, the first part of the above volume in a separate form, consisting of about 300 pages, entitled, " A Scriptural Answer to Dr. Pusey's Teaching on the Doctrine of the Real Presence, in which the Doctrines of the Lord's Supper as held by him, Roman Catholics, Ritualists, and High Anglo-Catholics are examined and shown to be contrary to the Holy Scriptures. Forming part of the volume by the same author entitled, An Answer to Dr. Pusey's Challenge respecting the Doctrine of the Real Presence, &c., consisting of the Scriptural portion of that Answer."

Price to Subscribers, Six Shillings.

Dr. Pusey, not only in his Eucharistic writings, but on several public occasions, has proclaimed with no faltering tongue his firm belief that his doctrines on the Lord's Supper are those of God's Word, and of the early Catholic Church. Having searched every nook and corner of antiquity with the aid of Roman Catholic Lights, he publishes the result in 400 pages of extracts from nearly 100 early Fathers, which he prefaces thus: " Some [passages of the Fathers] have been supplied from the originals recently published by Dom. Pitra and Card. Mai. It is remarkable that the single volume of Dom. Pitra should furnish three new early authorities. . . . The following evidence that the belief in the Real Presence was part of the faith of Christians from the first, is more than enough to convince one who is willing to be convinced. If this convince not, neither would any other. There is no flaw, no doubt, I might almost say, no loophole, except that man always finds one, to escape what he is unwilling to accept."—*Doctrine of the Real Presence, Notes, &c., pp.* 315-317. The same extracts he supplements as follows :—" I have suppressed nothing; I have not knowingly omitted anything; I have given every passage as far as in me lay, with so much of the context as was necessary for the clear exhibition of its meaning."—p. 715.

I have examined with enormous labour the whole of Dr. Pusey's leading Fathers, from whom he has made his extracts, and thoroughly examined about 1500 pages of his writings in relation to his peculiar doctrines on the Eucharist, and I think I can now prove to the ordinary reader who can weigh plain evidence, and has patience to do so, that Dr. Pusey's doctrines on the Eucharist are alike contrary to the Word of God and the teaching of the Catholic Church of the first eight centuries.

Although Dr. Pusey's writings on the Eucharist are very extensive, yet they are but fragmentary and incomplete, as he himself confesses. In order that the whole system of doctrine may be brought under examination, the lack in Dr. Pusey's writings will be supplemented from those of Dr. Wiseman, the late Bishop of Salisbury, Archdeacon Denison, the Rev. W. J. E. Bennett, the Rev. Orby Shipley, and the Rev. Gerard F. Cobb. In order that the arguments and illustrations of these men in favour of their doctrine may not be unfairly represented, they are given consecutively in their words, and will form about 60 pages of smaller type. From these extracts references will be made to those parts of the volume where any part of them is noticed. These extracts will be included in " A Scriptural Answer, &c.," noticed above. It should be here observed that although this part of the volume will contain more especially the Scripture arguments, yet where it seemed to suit my purpose I have freely quoted the choicest parts of the Fathers in confirmation of my interpretations, and more especially in refuting my opponents who accept them as binding authorities.

The most important part of the volume is the Catena Patrum, forming about 300 pages of smaller type. It consists of twenty witnesses, fifteen of which have been adduced by Dr. Pusey. These are Justin Martyr, Irenæus, Clement of Alexandria, Tertullian, Origen, Cyprian, Eusebius the Church historian, Cyril of Jerusalem, Basil, Ambrose, Jerome, Gaudentius, Augustine, Chrysostom, and Theodoret. That the reader may see how unfairly Dr. Pusey has quoted these witnesses and omitted the most important parts of their testimony (notwithstanding his assertion to the contrary), what has been quoted from Dr. Pusey's Catena will be printed in distinct type, so that garbled extracts, unfair translations, unaccountable omissions, &c. &c., will at once be made manifest. A few specimens are here given of a very large number. The portions printed in Italic type are quoted from Dr. Pusey's 400 pages of extracts from the Fathers, and the portions printed in Roman type, translated from the originals, form no part of Dr. Pusey's 400 pages, and are given to show how by omitting them he has in fact misrepresented the real sentiments of his witnesses.

CLEMENT OF ALEXANDRIA.

" Eat ye," He saith, " my flesh and drink my blood," and nothing is wanting, to the children's growth. O marvellous mystery! He bids us put off from us the old corruption of the flesh as also the old food, and partaking of another new nourishment, that of Christ, receiving Him as far as possible [if we can] *to lay Him up in ourselves and place the Saviour in our breast, that we may correct the passions of our flesh.*—pp. 328, 329. But you are not inclined to understand it thus, &c. . . . Let no one then think it strange when we say that the Lord's blood is figuratively represented as milk, for is it not figuratively represented as wine?

ORIGEN.

We enquire then how our Lord and Saviour, who is the true High Priest, with His disciples, who were true Priests, before He approacheth the altar of God, &c., p. 411. . . . Our Lord and Saviour says, "Except ye eat my flesh and drink my blood ye have no life in you, for my flesh is meat indeed, and my blood is drink indeed." . . . For with the flesh and blood of His own word, as with clean food and drink, He gives drink to and refits the whole race of men. In the second place, after the flesh of Him, Peter is clean food, and Paul, and all the Apostles. In the third place, the disciples, &c. . . . Not only in the Old Testament is the letter that killeth discovered; there is also in the New Testament a letter which killeth him who hath not perceived the things spiritually which are spoken. For if according to the letter thou followest, the thing itself where it hath been said, "Except ye eat my flesh and drink my blood;" this letter killeth.—(*Lev. Hom.* vii.)

But the Christian people, the faithful people, heareth these things and embraceth them, and followeth Him who saith: ' Except ye eat my flesh and drink my blood, ye have no life in you : for my flesh is meat indeed, and my blood is drink indeed.' And in truth He who said these things was wounded for men ; for ' He was wounded for our sins,' as Esaias saith. But we are said to drink the blood of Christ not only in the way of sacraments, but also when we receive His word [sermones, words] *in which is life as also Himself saith, ' The words which I speak unto you, they are spirit and they are life."*—p. 343. He therefore Himself has been wounded whose blood we drink, that is, we receive the words of His doctrine. But, nevertheless, they also have been wounded, who have preached to us His word, for we also read their words, that is, the words of His apostles ; and we who are following the life which is from them, drink the blood of the wounded. . . . *Thou then art the true people of Israel, which canst drink blood, and canst eat the flesh of the Word of God and drink His blood, and canst suck up the blood of that grape which is of the true vine, and of those branches which the Father purgeth.*—p. 344. The fruit of these branches is deservedly called the blood of those who are wounded, which we drink from their words and doctrine.

EUSEBIUS.

But understand well, that the words that I have spoken to you are spirit and life; so that His words and discourses are the flesh and blood of which he who always partakes, as one fed upon heavenly food, shall be a partaker of heavenly life.—*Contra Marcel, De Eccles. Theo. lib.* iii., *cap.* 12.

AUGUSTINE.

There must be care lest thou takest figurative language literally. For what the apostle said also appertains to this, "The letter killeth, but the spirit giveth life." For when that spoken figuratively is taken as if spoken properly, it is carnally tasted. . . . *Such as are the Sacrament of Baptism, and the celebration of the body and blood of the Lord.*—p. 509.

. . . If a form of speech is preceptive, forbidding either what is flagitious or horrible, or commanding what is useful or beneficent, it is not figurative, But if it seems to command what is flagitious or horrible, or forbid what is useful or beneficent, it is figurative. "Except ye eat the flesh and drink the blood of the Son of God, ye have no life in you." He seems to command what is horrible and flagitious ; therefore it is figurative commanding us to communicate in the passion of the Lord, and sweetly and profitably to treasure up in our memory that His flesh was crucified and wounded for us.

*So then the Eucharist is our daily bread; but let us in such receive it, that we be not refreshed in our stomach only but in our souls.—*p. 524. . . . Again, what I am hand-ling before you now is "daily bread;" and the daily lessons which you hear in church are " daily bread," and the hymns ye hear and repeat are "daily bread."

THEODORET.

As quoted and translated by Dr. Pusey.

As quoted and translated ~~from~~ the same edition.

ORTHODOX.—Thou knowest that God hath called bread His own body. ERAN-ISTES—I know it. ORTH.—And contra-rywise He hath called the flesh corn. ERAN. —I know this too, " Unless a corn of wheat fall into ground and die." ORTH.—But in instituting the mysteries He called the bread "body," and what is mingled "blood." ERAN.—He did so. ORTH.—But accord-ing to nature body would be called body; and blood, blood. ERAN. — Confessedly. ORTH.—But the Saviour interchanged the names; and to the body gave the name of the symbol, and to the symbol that of the body; so, having called Himself a vine, He entitled the symbol blood. ERAN.—Thou hast said truly. But I would know the cause of this change of names? . . . ORTH.— . . . For He who called the natural body corn and bread, and Himself again a vine, honoured the symbols which are seen with the title of bread and wine.—(T. iv. 25 ed. Sch.)

ORTH.—Do you not know that God called His proper body bread ? ERAN.—I know it. ORTH.—Elsewhere also He calleth His flesh wheat. ERAN.—I know that also : " Unless a corn of wheat fall into the ground and die," &c. ORTH.—But in the delivery of the mysteries, He called the bread His body, and that which is mixed blood. ERAN.—He did so call them. ORTH.—But that which is His body by nature, is also rightly called His body, and His blood (viz., by nature), blood. ERAN.—It is con-fessed. ORTH.—But our Saviour changed the names, and on His body He imposed the name of the symbol, and to the symbol He put the name of His body ; and so, having called Himself a vine, He called the symbol blood. ERAN.—Very right. But I have a mind to know the reason of the change of names ? . . . ORTH.— . . . For He that calleth His body, that is so by nature, wheat and bread, and again termed Himself a vine, He honoured the visible symbols with the title of His Body and Blood.

Dr Pusey has entirely omitted the testimony of Lactantius and Ruffinus, although these come within the dates to which he restricted himself. These I have added to his list with three others of a much later date, viz., Bede, who lived but a short time before the doctrine of the Real Presence in the consecrated elements was invented ; and Bertram and Rabanus Maurus, who lived at the time of its introduction by Paschasius, and both ably answered it, but especially the former. The doctrine of Paschasius, as stated by himself, will also be given. Where it is necessary, words and phrases will be given in the originals.

As far as patristic evidence is concerned, it is not at all necessary to quote all the fathers of antiquity to know what was generally held respecting the doctrine of the Lord's Supper. I contend that two, or three at most, are simply sufficient. If three are taken, let one be of the third century, one of the fourth, and one of the fifth century, and each the best reputed commentator and biblical scholar of the century in which he lived. Beyond all question these are Origen, Jerome, and Theodoret; and all that Dr Pusey has thought suitable for his purpose to quote from these authors is included in my Catena. I have not, however, confined myself to these witnesses, as the list shows. From Augustine alone I have quoted more than from all these three put together. Dr Pusey, happily, has given in his sermon what may be considered in his judgment the most valuable portions of his 400 pages of extracts from the fathers in a condensed form, and what he considers as best calculated to prove his doctrine. This will be given in full, and will be fairly examined.

The plan of the present is like that of the previously published volume, entitled : "Whose are the Fathers?" with the difference that in this, as has been noticed, the doctrinal statements of Dr Pusey and his school, will be printed in full in a separate por-tion of the book, and from it, as well as from the 350 pages of the *Catena Patrum* references will be made to those sections of the volume where the several parts are noticed and applied, so that the extracts from those whose doctrines are called in question, as well as the extracts from the Fathers. will form the text, and the volume will be the commentary upon it. The new work will, in fact, be a convenient and comprehensive, if not an exhaustive, text book on the Scripture and Patristic doctrine of sacraments more especially of that of the Lord's Supper.

The book will be got up in the same style as "Whose are the Fathers?" But the addition of marginal references will considerably increase the cost of printing. The price to subscribers for the entire volume, will be Twelve Shillings : and for the separate portion, as noticed above, Six Shillings. The author especially appeals to all those who take an interest in the controversy forced upon us, and hopes he shall have sufficient encouragement from subscribers to venture on publication, and if so, the book now nearly ready for the press, may be issued in three or four months. After the subscribers have been supplied, the volume will be published in the ordinary way, when the price will be considerably increased.

The subscriptions to be paid at the time of delivery. The names and addresses of subscribers may be sent to the author, the Rev. John Harrison, Vicar of Fenwick, Askern, near Doncaster.

EXTRACTS from Reviews of a Book Published by the same Author, entitled—

WHOSE ARE THE FATHERS? or the Teaching of Certain Anglo-Catholics on the Church and its Ministry, contrary alike to the Holy Scriptures, to the Fathers of the first Six Centuries, and to those of the Reformed Church of England. With a CATENA PATRUM of the first Six Centuries, and of the English Church of the latter half of the Sixteenth Century. Price 16s. London : Longmans, Green, & Co., and all Booksellers.

The Examiner.—Jan. 21, and March 9, 1867.

"The volume is an elaborate argument against High Church Episcopal pretensions founded on a theory of Apostolical Succession, which the author, the Rev. John Harrison, combats by turning the High Churchmen's guns, the Fathers of the first six centuries, against himself. Very learnedly, and at considerable length, Mr Harrison here investigates the writings of the early Christians, with the view of showing that their teachings give no sanction to the claims of the High Church party regarding the powers of the priesthood, and other questions of ecclesiastical government and discipline."

The Clerical Journal.—Feb. 7.

"Mr Harrison has added another volume to the many which have been lately written on each side of these great questions, and a marvellous volume it is, as displaying the learning, research, and industry of the author. He has compiled a book which would have tasked the energies of men enjoying 'the calm repose of the silent shade,' for quiet reading and academic advantages in the use of books. We do not pretend to have tested the correctness of these 740 pages, but they have a scholarly look, and the Greek and Latin are not to be found fault with. He goes about this work with a good heart, and every page makes us feel that he is in real earnest. His words often 'burn,' and he becomes eloquent in his indignant refutation of what he believes to be erroneous and mischievous. He has certainly convicted some among us of error, by the concurrent testimony of the Bible, the ancient Church, and our own Reformers. As a large collection of opinions and extracts, ancient and modern, the work will be highly useful for reference."

The Sheffield Daily Telegraph.—Feb. 23.

"Indeed, patristic theology is so ably handled in it, that, with every thoughtful reader, 'Whose are the Fathers?' will go a long way to remove that reproach of ignorance on that subject so freely, if not justly, cast upon Protestant divines. . . . And we are bound to add, also, that the writer has fulfilled his intention. . . . One knows not which to admire most in the writer, his learning, his patience of investigation, or the confidence with which he proceeds to attack every position of the enemy. A more thoroughly honest, patient, and painstaking book we have never seen."

Original Secession Magazine.—March and May.

"This is a work of no common merit. The author is a gentleman of great ability, discriminating judgment, and much learning. This volume is a magazine of information on the wide subject of which it treats. The results of the labours of Mr Harrison, contained in the pages of this work, make it manifest that he has a thorough acquaintance with the early history of the Christian Church, not at second-hand, but as the materials of this are furnished in the extant writings of the Fathers, in the Greek and Latin languages in which they were composed. These results are evidently the fruit of no ordinary labour, industry, and, in not a few cases, the investigation of recondite sources. Consisting largely as they do of facts, Mr Harrison's book will never be answered. . . . This volume is a treasure of information as to the sentiments and views of the Fathers of the Primitive Church. As a book of reference in these times, when such questions are likely to become, extensively, subjects of discussion, this work of Mr Harrison's will prove an acquisition of no ordinary value."

Sheffield and Rotherham Independent.—March 12.

"This book is a very elaborate and able production. The author justly considers that the Ritualistic practices and Romanizing tendencies of some portions of the clergy of the Church of England, have their origin in erroneous doctrines on the Church and its ministry. Accordingly, he sets himself in good earnest to show that these doctrines are not in accordance with Scripture, either as interpreted by the early Christian Fathers, or as expounded by the great Divines and Reformers of the English Church. It is due to the author to say that he has pursued his object with remarkable perseverance and toil. He had to seek for his materials in the voluminous writings of nearly sixty Latin and Greek authors, in nearly a hundred ponderous folios, and in most cases he had to make his own translations of such portions of their writings as bear upon this argument."

The Bulwark.—April.

"It is with peculiar delight that we have examined this singularly able and learned volume. No indication at the present moment can be more refreshing than that in the English Church a number of men are found, not only sound in the faith, but more than a match for any of the Ritualists in learning. We have no hesitation in saying that Mr Harrison, whose volume we have now before us, is one of this number; and we should reckon it a noble stroke of policy to convert him from being curate of Pitsmoor to being Professor of Protestant Theology at Oxford. We have little doubt he would prove himself, in such a position, if we may judge from the volume before us, to be more than a match for Dr Pusey and his allies. Mr Harrison accomplishes his task with singular clearness and the most ample and accurate learning. He exposes, in the most thorough and masterly way, the Popish figment of Apostolic Succession, and deals unsparingly with the literary credit of Dr Wordsworth, Mr Perceval, Dr Hook, the Bishop of Oxford, and others. The work will be found to be a perfect armoury of weapons to those who are anxious to vindicate the truth of God."

The London Quarterly Review.—April.

"The result is a comprehensive, learned, and almost exhaustive work of more than 700 octavo pages ; far more massy as a theological treatise, and far more likely to be permanent in its influence than its origin might have indicated. . . . The 300 pages of 'Catena,' consisting of careful quotations from the Fathers, from the early English Reformers, and from Divines of later date, are prepared with conscientious care and astonishing industry. The volume is well worth having for their sake alone ; but they are only adduced as illustration of an argument which seems, to our rapid glance at least, sound and clear. The book is beautifully printed, arranged with great skill, and furnished with a perfectly elaborated index."

The Journal of Sacred Literature.—April.

" This is an exceedingly good book, and likely enough to be useful in these days of ritual extravagance. . . . He has shown, by a very complete series of quotations, that the Anglo-Catholics are not justified in their very haughty assumptions of superiority, either by the Fathers of the Catholic or of the Anglican Church. He is quite successful in proving this. . . . We very heartily commend Mr Harrison's volume to all those persons on both sides of the great religious controversy, who really wish to know 'Whose are the Fathers?'"

British Quarterly Review.—April.

"Mr Harrison's book is a valuable magazine of patristic reference for combatants on his side the question. It meets the Ritualists on their own chosen ground, and although the oracle to which they appeal is not very congruous in its elements, Mr Harrison proves that, amid all the wild and self-contradictory theories of the Fathers, they do not teach Apostolical Succession. This he does with candour, considerable scholarship, and conclusive argumentation."

United Presbyterian Magazine.—May.

" The ample title-page gives one a very good idea of this volume ; and the author has made out his cause in a very exhaustive manner. . . . The volume now before us is a treasury of reference on this subject nowhere else to be found ; and immense must have been the labour and research employed in its preparation. The extracts are generally given with such fulness of the context as to determine the meaning. We have verified a number of them, and have found them correct."

The Athenæum.—May 25.

"When Job wished that his adversary had written a book, it was said before books of reference were in existence. He did not contemplate an opponent collecting dry facts or opinions against him, with an index. Such a compiler may expose his opponent, but cannot expose himself, until he is convicted of absolute fraud, or fraudulent carelessness. The Rev. John Harrison is in this position. He has struck a blow at the High Church principle, which must tell, unless he can be convicted of either suppression or mistranslation, and even if he should have wilful suppression brought home to him, no matter what the amount, his dictionary of quotations retains all its power as a book on one side of the question ; while the corresponding book on the other side, if it can be got together, will only make Kilkenny cats of the Fathers, and finish the controversy in that way. In the meanwhile, if the volume before us be fairly done, it has a dictionary life, and a slow and permanent dictionary effect. It gets into the quiet country library, and is used for many a year against the 'little book of nonsense'—as Sydney Smith called it—which the ritualist curate lends to the daughters of the possessor, until at last the poor young ladies have nothing for it, but 'Oh! papa! that's a Harrison!'

"Both sides are given : that is, all the passages of each Father which bear upon the subject, whether they wish to oppose or to favour the succession. Thus we find a sentence of Jerome, on which Dr Wiseman laid great stress, given in three ways : Dr Wiseman's version ; Mr Harrison's version : and the original."

From a Private Letter of Dean Woods, May 28th 1867.

" The importance of the subject, and the labour and care which Mr Harrison has evidently bestowed upon the work, will, he has no doubt, make it a valuable contribution to our ecclesiastical literature."

The Watchman.—June 5.

" We are thankful to the author of this exhaustive treatise for his laborious research, perfect candour, and triumphant refutation of the sophistries which would 'make the Word of God of none effect,' and undo the work of the Reformation. This is truly a book which deserves the thoughtful perusal of all who care that 'the foundations' of our Protestant faith should not be 'destroyed.' The question treated in this large, and yet concise volume is one to which no well-instructed Christian can be indifferent. . . . He hardly could have rendered a greater service to the age than thus to meet a spurious Anglicanism with its own weapons."

"Mr Harrison has fixed upon one point in the Tractarian controversy, namely, the dogma of apostolic succession, and he has sifted the whole question from an historical point of view, with considerable acumen, giving us, in one manageable volume, the results of researches which must have extended over a very large field. . . . He seems to be well acquainted with all that the High-Anglicans have written on the subject, and in the course of his arguments he exposes the astonishing mis-quotations and mis-statements which such learned men as Dean Hook, and even Archdeacon Wordsworth, have been led into by a prejudiced judgment or by the heat of controversy. . . . We hope that Dr Hook will study Mr Harrison's work before issuing a new edition of his *Church Dictionary* —a most unsatisfactory book. Amongst other things, he will have to amend his article on the 'Bidding Prayer,' in which he endeavours to prove that the 'Presbyterian Establishment' of Scotland is not a Church. . . . We think Mr Harrison has thoroughly succeeded in proving that the early Fathers are by no means in favour of that form of apostolic succession which was advocated in the 'Tracts for the Times,' and which is at the root of the priestly pretensions of the Ritualists. . . . Mr Harrison's own views of Episcopacy are sound and just, and are in accordance both with Scripture and with the teaching of the Reformers. . . . A careful study of the Patristic writings will lead the honest inquirer to the conclusion, that the dogma of apostolic succession, as held by the Bishop of Oxford and Dr Hook, was not even known to the majority of the Fathers."

The British and Foreign Evangelical Review.—July.

"We are bound to say that Mr Harrison has done his work most thoroughly. His book is an exhaustive one on the subject to which it relates. He gives the teaching of the Anglo-Catholics in their own words, examines their quotations from the Fathers, and, with a perfect mastery over his subject, points out how unfairly they have dealt even with their own authorities, which, if honestly quoted and justly interpreted, ought to have led them to opposite conclusions. There will not be found in this work any rhetorical artifices. His style is quiet and unassuming, but there is from one end of his argument to the other, a manly straightforwardness, and a consciousness of power, which proves strangely attractive to those who have an interest in such researches. But that which ought to secure for his volume a place in the library of every one who is concerned in the Episcopal controversy, is the valuable ' *Catena Patrum,*' which occupies the latter part of it. Our readers will easily gather, from the specimen given in these pages [16 pp.] some idea of the valuable contribution which Mr Harrison has made to the Episcopal controversy, and they will find, also, that the author is well acquainted with Greek, Hebrew, and Syriac, though his learning is never obtrusively pressed on their attention."

The Freeman.—July 5.

"It is a book for students, and forms an admirable dictionary of quotations on theological and ecclesiastical subjects. Those students and general readers who have not sufficient means to purchase the works of the Fathers, nor ability to read them in the original tongue, may turn to it with very great advantage. . . . Mr Harrison must have laboured hard in the composition of this volume. The research involved in the production of these quotations must have been immense. The reader is reminded of the days and controversies of the Puritans, when Charnock produced copious selections from the ancients, to illustrate or enforce some view of the 'attributes,' and when Jeremy Taylor crowded his margins with the most striking sayings of Chrysostom and Augustine. Mr Harrison has done his work in a thorough and scholar-like manner; he has not gathered his passages from second-hand authorities, but has, in almost all instances, gone to the original sources, and has even given, in important quotations, the various renderings, Popish and Protestant."

Church and State Review.—March 2.

"The ' Catena Patrum ' must have cost him a considerable amount of patient toil, as well as of time; and there are traces throughout the book of wide and various reading."

The Ecclesiastic.—May.

"We think Mr Harrison is deserving of great credit for the lucid arrangement of his book. It is well and carefully put together; the 'Catena' applying clearly to and explaining the text. We sympathize with Mr Harrison in long work and literary labour, and he and his sect may justly take some pride in the book."

The Church Review.—April 20 and 27.

"The arrangement and method of the book are capital, and the application of the 'Catena' to the text is excellently managed. We find long extracts from the Fathers of the Church collected with considerable care, and fairly translated."

The Homilist.—December.

"Mr Harrison has spared no pains, and he has brought together every thing which industry, scholarship, research, and a keen intellect could suggest to make it worthy of its high aim. . . . We have had before us a very large number of publications on the Ritualistic question, some of them being marked by much learning and ability. We incline to the belief that the work now before us will be of more permanent service than even the best."

Reformed Presbyterian Magazine.—October.

"This is truly a notable volume, by no means to be lost sight of in the extensive literature of modern controversies. It has peculiar claims on the attention of those who would study thoroughly the questions to which it relates. It is a storehouse of facts and arguments, collected with great research and stated in a way vivid, clever, and impressive, without the least trace of affectation and pretence. The book is the result of great labour and care. The argument to High Church theories is close and exhaustive. The discussion is conducted, from chapter to chapter, with sustained vigour and animation. The author depends not on the strength of his language, but the value and relevancy of his facts. He, nevertheless, has the gift of so marshalling his facts and putting his case, that the reader never feels his interest flagging in the searching exposure of the untenableness of High Church claims.

Biblical Notes and Queries.

"We cannot sufficiently commend to those of our readers who feel an interest in the subject, this elaborate and scholarly work. Printer, Publisher, and author have done their best."

The Rock.—August 10th 1869.

"The whole work is literally a monument of the author's learning, sagacity, and industry. . . . The main object of this learned compiler is like that of Hannibal of old, who carried the war into the country of the enemy, showing, as he does, that the Scriptural quotations made by the Ritualists in their defence are either not at all to the point or else condemnatory of their own principles, and that their interpretations of Scripture are either refuted by their own canons of interpretation, or by the voice of Christian antiquity and tradition, to which they are so very fond of appealing. The refutation of the Bishop of Oxford's views and those of Dr. Hook on this question is convincing in the extreme."

By the Same Author.

AN ANTIDOTE to the teaching of certain Anglo-Catholics concerning Worshipping Eastward, "Altar" Adoration, Clerical Sacerdotalism, Baptism, and the "Real Presence," with an Exposure of the Assumption that their Religion is "The Bible interpreted by the Church." Pages 48. Price 1s.—Longmans, Green & Co., London.

"The title really tells us what the treatise proposes to do, and what it really does. We wish we could influence some layman who loves the Scriptural Church of England, to order a still cheaper edition of this 'Antidote,' and send it to all the clergy in the land."—*Our Own Fireside.*

"A vigorous and well-written antidote. . . . Its array of authorities possesses features of permanent interest."—*The Record.*